In memory of Michael and Dora King

I have desired to go
Where springs not fail,
To fields where flies no sharp and sided hail
And a few lilies blow.

Gerard Manley Hopkins, from 'A Nun Takes the Veil'

Her head was a jumble of coffin mountings and funeral wreaths when Sister Deirdre Logan struggled to turn off the alarm clock. Like a swimmer in the grip of an undertow, she panicked for a moment as she failed to rise above the surface of her troubled dream. Two minutes before, or so it seemed, she had rested her head on the pillow. The smell of varnished death had invaded her room. She reached for the comforting bedside light, but then the bizarre images of the night gave way to a grim reality: today Ita will be buried.

The nuns from the country towns who were staying overnight in Oak Hill had chatted in the community room until well after midnight; when they met in the corridors they spoke in hushed tones. They took turns keeping vigil in the chapel, where the dead nun lay in an open coffin. The only light came from tall candles flickering in front of the sanctuary. Deirdre and those who were part of Ita's group in the noviciate had had a last run through the lessons and hymns for the Requiem Mass. Along with that, she had been checking to see that they had soap and towels, and enough blankets.

While she was putting on her dressing gown, fragments from the evening seeped into her sluggish thoughts: the sheen on the hearse crawling beneath the street lights outside the mortuary, the archbishop reciting prayers in the crowded chapel, and afterwards, the way he had kept calling her Sister Mary Ita. 'I'm Sister Deirdre,

Your Grace,' she had reminded him. The blue-rinsed heads of those she hadn't seen since the last Assembly three years before also figured in her reverie.

In the way of her convent training, she banished these troublesome pictures with activity: tidying the room, which was just big enough for her bed, a bookcase, a desk and a fireside chair. Beside a built-in press was Ita's weekend bag, containing what the nurse in St Vincent's called 'her personal effects' – a blue nightdress, underwear, a John Le Carré novel and a Walkman. The bag still gave off a hospital smell. She turned away and concentrated on the sheet music for the Mass.

Oak Hill began to stir itself: taps croaked and water gurgled from basins. Padded footsteps hurried along the corridor. Next door, Joan put away a Mills and Boon and began to clear her throat – a habit that ceased only while she managed two or three hours' sleep. But what had often been an irritant for Deirdre now became a cushion against sickness and the sight of curtains drawn around yet another bed. And the hospital chaplain reciting the final prayers before death: this had been a feature of her life for the previous three months while she'd visited her friend.

When light began to filter through the roller blind, she stood and reached over the desk to pull the cord. The green dome of Rathmines Church caught her eye. Away to the right a wind from Siberia was scattering smoke from the Pigeon House chimneys. A seagull skimmed the earth in search of food and glided off in the direction of the cemetery. The weather report the night before had predicted that the cold spell would continue: temperatures had dropped lower than those of '69, the last time the lake had frozen over. That was the year the heating had broken down in the noviciate and the postulants had had to move to the Academy Hall while a new boiler was being installed.

SWAN SONG

WILLIAM KING

Acknowledgements

The author and publisher would like to thank the following for permission to quote extracts from various works: Random House UK Ltd for 'Birches' by Robert Frost; Faber and Faber Ltd for 'East Coker' and 'Dry Salvages', both from *Four Quartets,* in *Collected Poems 1909–62* by T. S. Eliot, and an extract from 'This Be the Verse' from *Collected Poems* by Philip Larkin; Veritas Pubications Dublin for permission to quote from the Roman Catholic funeral rites.

Like prints dipped in photographic solution, the images from that overcast day nearly thirty years before began to develop in her mind as she stood gazing at the polished lake. She heard again the clank of metal as the novices, working in pairs, dismantled the bedsteads. And Ita making French beds by turning up the bottom sheet halfway in someone else's bed – a practical joke they played on each other as soon as the finger-snapping novice mistress had gone out the door.

The sheet music blurred. She closed the folder and made her way through the dim corridor where the smell of hot iron rose from the ancient radiators. In the chapel, she knelt at her place beside the organ.

From time to time others entered – mostly the older ones who had shuffled across from the nursing home – and added to the whisper of prayers. One or two went up and touched the coffin and then returned to their prie-dieu.

She opened her breviary, but all she saw was Ita's wasted body in the hospital bed and her desperate appeal: 'Is this all there is? Is this it?' She had been cheated, she cried. 'A stupid notion of giving up everything for God. Thérèse of Lisieux. A child's fantasy fed by silly nuns in a convent school. Well, what's He doing for me now?' All Deirdre could do was hold her hand on the coverlet.

Another day, Ita had blamed her aunt, the nun who used to visit every summer, leaving behind a clean convent smell and a ticket of admission to heaven. And for a while then, she was an eight-year-old Sister Ita going around the kitchen or out to the bar with a towel around her head, and her mother's rosary beads hanging from the belt of her dress. Her father hid his whiskey behind the counter and laughed with the men who were putting up poles for the Electricity Supply Board.

When she had spent her anger, she drifted into a drugged

sleep while Deirdre kept vigil. 'Don't leave me,' Ita had pleaded, 'it's less frightening if you're there when I wake.'

After Matins, de Chantal walked beside Deirdre to the refectory. 'Poor Ita,' de Chantal said. 'Long before her time. I remember the day you both entered – the feast of the Holy Rosary.' She fumbled for a handkerchief. 'God's will.'

'God's will, de Chantal.'

To make room for the extra numbers, the kitchen staff and old Eddie the caretaker had brought tables and chairs from the storeroom. Conversation flowed as if they were celebrating a feast day. They had taken their cue from the archbishop: 'Sister Mary Ita embodied God's goodness to mankind. Her funeral will be a way of giving thanks to the Almighty.'

Some of the older nuns still retained the navy habit and black veil; the rest were middle-aged women in smart suits or matching skirts and jackets. They wore earrings and had had their hair done the day before.

'Didn't she look so peaceful,' said Joan at the side table, where they served themselves from a range of cereals, juice and fruit. 'I mean, really peaceful, as if she were asleep,' she continued, as they sat down. 'And like a schoolgirl – so young. Don't you think so?'

'Exactly,' a nun beside her agreed. The others nodded and exchanged knowing looks: Joan was high again.

A sharp tinkle silenced the chat. Sister Emmanuel, the Superior General, seated beneath a picture of Catherine Browne, the founder, welcomed the visitors and wished they had been meeting in happier circumstances. Then, Rita, who had control of the bell, popped up and let them know about seating arrangements for the funeral, and about the reception after-wards. In addition to her duties as Superior of Oak Hill, she was also bursar-general to the congregation and had, as many of the Sisters suspected, her sights set on the top post when Emmanuel returned to the missions.

As soon as Deirdre noticed the procession of priests at the door of the chapel, she nodded to the choir and touched the keys of the organ for the opening hymn. The congregation stood and joined in.

> *God fills me with joy, alleluia,*
> *His holy presence is my robe, alleluia*
> *My soul now glorify the Lord, who is my saviour.*

The altar server's swaying thurible discharged a cloud of smoke that glided towards the dark beams of the vaulted ceiling and filled the church with the spiced odour of incense that would linger long after the funeral was over. At the foot of the altar, the concelebrants fanned out at each side of the chaplain. All had links with Oak Hill: Ita's spiritual director from Manresa, a priest who had a sister in the community and another priest, Millar, who had a reputation for having a nun in every convent in Dublin and kissed the altar with remarkable devotion. Head and shoulders above the rest was Richard O'Brien, who had been a favourite for convent retreats while he lectured in All Saints Seminary. Deirdre glanced at the organ mirror: Aidan Doyle looked tired – probably playing cards until all hours.

They had been checking the classrooms to see that everything was in order after the summer holiday when Ita broke the news. Crossing by the hockey pitch, Deirdre indicated the dormitories – a grey building to the side of the convent.

'Hard to believe it will be all gone next year,' Deirdre said.

'Time marches on,' Ita said in return, not bothering to look up.

'An apartment block, I believe.'

Ita kept on walking.

In the refectory they made tea. Night was falling. 'I've no intention of taking on the same workload as last year,' Deirdre said, taking a milk jug out of the fridge. 'We're not getting any younger.' She meant it. Preparing the Leaving Certificate classes was enough, she was about to say, when she spotted Ita leaning against the worktop, her head sunk between her shoulders.

'What's wrong?' she asked and rushed to Ita's side. 'Is it migraine again?'

'A lump.' The click of the kettle went unheeded. 'In the shower. Yesterday.'

'It may only be a cyst.'

'No.' Ita shook her head. 'It was the same with Mother. Tired all the time. You remember?'

'But even if it were – you know – in any way sinister . . .' Deirdre hesitated. 'They've been making great progress, not like in the past.'

The chaplain was speaking about her strong faith. A faith that was sown in a good Catholic home and was later nourished in another family – the Sisters of the Precious Blood. He used his well-worn verse:

> *For though from out our borne of time and place*
> *The flood may bear me far,*
> *I hope to see my pilot face to face*
> *When I have crossed the bar.*

But she lost him again to the scene in the cancer ward when the nuns had started to pray: 'Thank you, Jesus, thank you for everything you've done for Ita. Praise you, Jesus. Praise you, Jesus.'

'Shut up,' Ita cried. 'Shut up and go away. I'm dying and all you can do is say prayers. Go away and take these stupid relics with you.' A pale hand swept the novenas off the bedcover.

Visitors were reassuring their dying relatives: 'You look much better than you did yesterday.' But the commotion from inside the curtained bed caused the bogus chatter to founder. They threw sidelong glances at the chaplet of Sister Faustina, lying on the polished floor, and then, with their grapes and Lucozade in Tesco bags beside them, they continued to bolster up: 'And you'll dance at the wedding. Of course you will.'

The day before she died, a blush returned to her cheeks. She spoke of her readiness to meet God. The old nuns were delighted: they resumed their drone of litanies.

*

Her spiritual director said the Prayer of Final Commendation while the chaplain swung the thurible around the coffin:

> *May the angels lead you into Paradise, Ita,*
> *May the martyrs come to welcome you*
> > *And take you to the Holy City,*
> > *The new and eternal Jerusalem.*
> *Whoever believes in me, even though that person dies, shall live.*

The priests led the cortège down the centre aisle while the choir sang *'Confitemini Domino.'* Outside, vicious hailstones bit at their legs. One nun kept a gloved hand on her veil until they reached the shelter of the cypress hedge.

'Give our sister peaceful rest in this grave,' the chaplain read. 'Look with compassion on your servants who are sorely grieved by their loss.' Ice pellets jigged on the coffin and came to rest on the silver plate.

The friends of Oak Hill stayed for lunch in the Long Parlour. With glasses of whiskey and sherry, they stood in clusters and exchanged anecdotes about how good Ita was to her pupils. She killed herself working: organising trips every Easter and putting on plays at Christmas. And they could phone her at any hour. Soon the litany of praises became threadbare and the conversation moved on to the great work of the Precious Blood Sisters.

Beside the stone fireplace stood the local GP and his wife, along with a politician and the schools inspector. They had discovered a shared interest in the cornices and the floral motifs of rococo-style design: the mahogany table and the lacquered screens dated back to Benjamin Russell, who had built the mansion in the nineteenth century. The schools inspector was able to fill them in on other details, such as the French ebony writing desk brought by Catherine Browne from Belgrave, her dower house. While doing inspections of Precious Blood schools, the inspector had been to dinner on several occasions at Oak Hill, so he was able to give them titbits about mirrors, brass fenders and the Venetian glass chandelier now catching the flames from the fire. The chaplain, a young man with a ring, joined them but had to be excused. Word came that his BMW was in someone's way. While keeping up with the party talk, the doctor's wife, a blonde-haired woman, stole glances at herself in the overmantel.

The forecast had been correct. Snow was beginning to fall as the nuns who were last to leave the grave gained the shelter of the Doric pillars: they shook powder from their shoulders and stamped their feet outside the front door.

'Deirdre,' one of the teachers called as she was hurrying up the steps. 'My sympathy.' In a mannered way, he held her hand in both of his. Ever since the staff party of the previous Christmas he had been avoiding her. But not that night.

'What's a fine-looking woman like you doing in a convent?' he had asked her after several drinks in the Braemor Rooms. 'A waste.' His lazy grin and shock of dark hair were disarming, but she tried to change the subject. 'I was too young, Deirdre,' he persisted. 'Shouldn't have got married so soon out of Maynooth.' His objective after three years in the seminary, he lamented, was to have a job, a wife and a house within a year.

In the Long Parlour and along the corridor, waitresses, carrying silver trays of whiskey and sherry, drifted between the clusters. Past pupils embraced nuns they hadn't seen since their own daughters had been at Oak Hill. They were sorry to hear the boarding school was to come under the hammer.

Rita flitted around, sprinkling pleasantries and taking words of sympathy in her stride. One woman commented on her figure: 'Like a teenager, if you don't mind my saying so, Sister.' Rita laughed it off and joined Moloney, the auctioneer, who was arranging the sale of a plot of land along by Mill Road. Aidan Doyle's cigar smoke hung in the crowded corridor, where he was in conversation with a few nuns who were reminiscing about the old days and telling him he was the best chaplain they had ever had.

'And you should never have left us, Father Aidan,' one of them said.

'Had to answer the summons, Sister.' His roguish eye sifted through the gathering until he spotted Deirdre. He excused himself and called her. Aware that their every move was being parsed, he shook her hand and offered a few hackneyed comments about the funeral. Turning away from the nuns, he lowered his voice: 'I've to jolly along these old dears. I'll ring you during the week.' He winked.

Having spent five years in his first appointment as emigrant chaplain in London, Aidan had arrived at Oak Hill to say the seven-thirty Mass each morning and hear the nuns' confessions. As a novice, Deirdre had served him his rasher and egg in the parlour – that was just after the Vatican Council when the lifeline John XXIII had offered to convents and seminaries was beginning to reach the Precious Blood Sisters. A couple of years later Aidan had started taking herself and Ita out to Dalkey or across to Howth in his red Volkswagen.

The day they had cast off the names allotted to them at first profession, he took them for a meal to Wynn's and afterwards to a play at the Abbey. Deirdre was no longer Germanus, Ita no longer Mary Paul. 'No doubt who Aidan has set his cap at,' said

Ita, when they were both reviewing the evening over a cup of tea in the refectory.

In one of the side parlours off the main door a group of nuns, Deirdre's contemporaries, had brought their plates and wineglasses to a quiet corner. These nuns were the remnant of those who had flown the nest after the Vatican Council. At the beginning, when veils and habits were cast aside, they had made do with hand-me-downs from their families and presents from their pupils' parents.

'Like strays from *Tenko*,' de Chantal had quipped, comparing their attire to a prisoner-of-war series that was on television around that time. Now they were a cluster of well-dressed women in their middle years. Whenever he gave a retreat, Father Aengus OFM, known as the Devil-at-Dances Priest because of his obsession with the evils of the ballroom, used to call them the 'flower of Irish womanhood'. They had aged well.

Rita joined them, but had to leave soon afterwards when she heard Moloney was putting on his coat.

'Duty calls, girls,' she said, brushing imaginary specks off her skirt.

'Yes, duty,' said one, when she had gone. 'Of course, Rita is a Three in the Enneagram.'

'With a wing in a Six.'

'Sixes like to be in charge.' They laughed.

For a while they had sworn by the Enneagram, a benign reading of personality traits that had replaced the charismatic renewal meetings in Halston Street – the nearest they got then to a night out on the town. Each Friday they had hopped on a bus and sampled the sweet taste of freedom for the first time. Good old John XXIII. From charismatic prayer they graduated to the Inner Me, encounter groups and workshops on self-discovery. And in a high tide of sharing with priests and brothers, they jettisoned the traditional counsels to perfection. The Enneagram, the younger generation agreed, was a wonderful help in mutual understanding and for spending 'quality time' together. A sister's number was a key to overlooking her defects. 'Matchmaking weekends' was what one old nun called them.

Deirdre had lunch with Ita's family. Here, the fall in vocations and the sale of the boarding school provided a respite from praising the choir and the sermon. All the while, the family were keeping a watchful eye on the bachelor brother whenever he reached for another whiskey.

Eventually, the gloom through the high windows got them moving for scarves and coats. Rita was at hand to help. They steeled themselves for a final parting at the main door. Ita's aunt, who had celebrated her ninetieth birthday two years before, was anxious to get back to her convent: in a timorous voice, she kept reminding them of the weather forecast. 'She is praying for us now in heaven,' she said, as they helped her down the steps.

Already the ground was turning white. Beneath umbrellas, they reminded each other of the month's mind Mass: it made parting easier. Then, sheltered by the portico, the nuns waved until the cars had disappeared, leaving two dark furrows in the driveway.

'The rest will be gone soon,' Rita said, in little more than a whisper, and indicated the open door of the Long Parlour. 'Thank God,' she added, between her teeth.

A novice – the only one they had received in the last four years – was struggling with a tray of glasses on her way to the kitchen. 'I'll give you a hand with them,' Deirdre offered.

'No,' Rita cut in, 'you've done more than enough already. Take a rest and we'll have a chat after tea.' She brushed her hand along

Deirdre's shoulder. 'It can't have been easy for you to play at the Mass.'

'OK, then.'

Alone in her room, she slumped into the easy chair. The dark lintel above her window showed up the swarm of snowflakes, like feathers set free from some enormous duvet in the sky. They dashed against the panes of glass, dissolved into liquid and slid down the window. Words of farewell and more reminders of the month's mind Mass reached her. Rita's tinny voice: 'Thanks a mill'.' She grew drowsy, removed her shoes and lay on the bed.

One image got entangled in another as her concentration lapsed. The undertakers were letting down the coffin again, holding the strap with one hand and paying out with the other, knees bent to balance the weight until the soft landing on a bed of straw. Joan in tears. The laughing chaplain on his way up the path after the funeral.

'No!' she called out. 'No! No! Not dead. Not yet.' She woke herself and took a second to shake off the dream. The room had grown dark, but the ceiling was unusually bright.

She was alive. Thank God. Not in a coffin, as she had dreamt. Rita and Hannah and other nuns were lowering her into the grave. Her mother was sprinkling holy water. 'But I'm alive,' she cried. They couldn't hear. She called to Dad. He would stop them. But he was in the distance, talking and laughing with other men.

She raised herself off the bed to pull down the blind, but stopped to look out at the snow-covered roofs. A gust of wind caused a slide in the evergreens and a cloud of white dust rose when the drift hit the surface of the lake.

The cold spell lasted for about two more weeks, and then, one Friday morning, spring and the first attack of examination fever showed up at Oak Hill. And instead of keeping to the resolution she had made to Ita about lessening her workload, Deirdre took more groups for tuition than ever before, so that she returned to the convent each evening just in time for tea. After Vespers she had copies to correct, classes to prepare or choir practice in the parish church, where she directed the singing at the 11.30 Mass. Saturday mornings she did her laundry and helped de Chantal with the plants in the glass corridor leading to the nursing home. And in this way she almost succeeded in dulling the pain of her loss.

But sometimes she woke in the far reaches of the night and stared at two hours of tossing and turning ahead of her, wrestling with cancer and graves and the loss of her friend. On those occasions, she found herself siding with the old convent rule that banned particular friendships: keep at a distance from everyone and death can be cheated. No highs or lows. But that style of thinking brought on a wave of guilt: Ita had always been there for her. She, above anyone else, had challenged Deirdre's starchy ways.

At times too she caught herself looking forward to their Sunday walk up in Glencullen, or when she saw a film advertised in the newspaper. Her mind raced ahead: they would go at the weekend. The daydream crash-landed on Ita's grave. Common sense deserted her. There's neither rhyme nor reason to the world, she thought. All a matter of chance. Her anger turned on Ita: why didn't she take more care of her health? Always running around: school work, youth discos and cookery classes in the community centre. What was she trying to prove? And worrying about that drunken brother of hers. No wonder she was so thin. And those migraine attacks. Weren't doctors nowadays saying that cancer is brought on by stress? The orbit of her tormenting thoughts around death and the loss of Ita ended only in self-reproach and a headache.

Whenever these brooding reflections slipped through the barrier of her busy days she began to see the vast empty spaces of Oak Hill. Especially so over weekends, when those who were teaching or doing retreat work had a variety of excuses for being away. Hannah had to look after her sick mother, who was so often at death's door; yet soon after one of these crises, they were spotted together feeding the ducks in St Stephen's Green. Every Friday she took possession of the Nissan; on the back window she had put a sticker: 'Grow Your Own Dope – Plant a Man'. 'Better remove that, Hannah,' Rita advised her. 'It doesn't look right on a convent car.' She replaced it with one that read: 'Zero Tolerance for Violence Against Women.'

The elderly nuns shuffled around the cloister saying their rosary if the day was fine; others dozed in front of the TV or devoured romantic novels. Deirdre lent John McGahern's *Amongst Women* to one of them, but she returned it the following day with a milky smile: 'Too much like what I'm trying to forget, Deirdre. Danielle Steele or Jeffrey Archer – they're more my cup of tea.' Anselm read the agony columns and gave a detailed account of each letter at supper. In fine weather, those who were able trudged around the walled garden with their nieces, while children threw pebbles into the dried-up fountain.

Some of the children had found a new lease of life through playing Solitaire on the computer. 'PlayStation – their second childhood,' de Chantal had quipped. The three computers were occupied every evening and those who were teaching couldn't get a chance to do their data processing after school.

Deirdre was washing one morning when she discovered red, scaly patches on her shoulder: the dreaded psoriasis that had made its first appearance the year she entered, and again before her final profession. She went to the convent doctor, who wrote out a prescription and, with an arm around her shoulder, told her not to be worrying about her vocation – and that she was a great nun.

She had come safely through storms before: when she had been a novice and her father was dying, but she wouldn't be allowed visit him until near the end. 'Our heavenly Father takes care of us all, Sister Germanus,' the Reverend Mother had told her. She had suffered her share of humiliation in the name of spiritual formation as well. 'Remember,' the novice mistress said, giving her a dressing down one morning, 'just because you shine at university is no reason to think you will be a good nun. And Oak Hill girls think they will be treated differently. Not while I'm in charge. Pride is one of the seven deadly sins.' After Vatican II, she had endured the energy-sapping arguments over veils and the length of habits, and still remained when her friends packed their suitcases and departed while everyone else was at chapel. But she was young then, and wrapped up in serving God, teaching and upholding the high reputation of the Precious Blood Sisters: nearly every year they ranked among the schools with the highest number of honours.

At meals, only passing references were made to Ita: funny incidents, like the time she dressed up as the Superior General and gave a talk to the newly arrived postulants while the novice mistress was away. But she was with the Lord, so there was no place for grief. Life had to go on.

She could have taken up Aidan Doyle's dinner invitation. 'Now that I'm in the south side we'll be able to meet more often,' he had said when he came to the month's mind. She strolled with him to the front door, where they stood talking.

'You should move out of here, Deirdre. This place gives me the creeps. Only for geriatrics. Go to one of the small communities out in the estates.' He thought for a moment. 'I'll get tickets for the Concert Hall. It will cheer you up.'

'Not next week – I'm busy with the Leaving Certs.'

She tilted her head. His slip-on shoe with its gold bridge-strap was resting on the iron foot-scraper. He had a ready answer for everything. But he meant well; nevertheless, she was wary. And she was determined to avoid a return to the nights when they had both lost control in his sitting room.

Before he left, he rooted beneath a golfing umbrella and racing cards in the back seat of his car. Thrown beside them were copybooks, faded and curling under the light. He didn't have the heart to refuse young blokes who hawked them at traffic lights. 'I brought you something from the Canaries,' he said, handing her a box containing a Lladrò figurine wrapped in tissue paper.

After school one evening, she lingered with de Chantal over a cup of tea. The graveyard stillness evoked memories of the past, and speculation about the future of Oak Hill. De Chantal had seen another convent in the newspaper's property section that day. In a leisurely way, they set themselves a test of naming the sisters who had occupied the vacant places: the nun who had married a local curate; the two who had left together and set up house in

Churchtown. They counted the numbers who had died in the previous years. Rita joined them and was sipping a glass of warm water. She affected sympathy but was called away to the phone. Then they heard her in the corridor: 'No, Sister Joan is not here.' And a shriek. 'Take those hockey sticks off the polished floor! Remember you are Oak Hill girls.' A door banged.

De Chantal smiled, removed her glasses and raised a spindly hand to rub her dark eyes. When she had been a young nun in charge of the dormitory, the girls made up stories to explain to themselves why someone so lovely should have entered a convent. She must have been engaged to a handsome doctor who had got killed in a road accident. They copied her handwriting.

'You're not yourself,' Deirdre heard her say, when she had replaced the glasses.

'Resurrection and heaven and God. And all I can think of is Ita lying in a grave long before her time. Only yesterday I was looking over the Mass booklet. All the hymns – "God Fills Me with Joy" – as if we were at a jubilee.'

The invitation to talk brought on a surge of feeling, but she tried for a while to hold back the tears. 'The saddest funeral of all can be a nun's – or a priest's. No spouse, no children. And everyone going on about how she is with the Lord – praying for us.'

Remarkably nimble for her years, de Chantal closed the refectory door.

'So much has been going on.' Deirdre stopped crying. 'Inside, I mean. Sad one minute, then angry the next. And thoughts. I can't make sense out of it. Like something out of control.' She inspected her nails. 'And going over to that hospital. I can't pray. Not a single word.'

'More honest than the platitudes.'

'It isn't just Ita's death alone.'

'No?'

'Life. My own life.' She hesitated. 'Even God.' She recalled a woman who had been in the bed opposite Ita. 'I was there the evening she got her hairpiece and I held the mirror while she fitted it on. Her only concern was to be alive for her son's First Communion. She died the week before Christmas.' Deirdre had joined the family for prayers. Across the corridor, in the sluice room, Shane McGowan was singing 'Fairy Tale of New York'. While preparing the body for the mortuary, one of the nurses picked up a crumpled card off the bedspread: a picture of Alan Shearer the little boy had brought to show his mammy. 'All the way home I couldn't get that little boy out of my head. It was unfair. Cruel. Surely if there's a God . . . ' Her voice trailed off.

She examined her nails. 'I'm kept going by day. But when I wake at four or five and I can't hide anywhere, I'm asking myself silly questions: Is she cold? And I'm remembering the day she said in Vincent's, "Get out, Deirdre, while you still have time".'

'But she was delirious then.'

'Maybe.' She straightened out a pleat in her skirt. 'When I can't get back to sleep, I take out Augustine's *Confessions*. Half of his soul was lost, he says, when his friend died. I wouldn't go that far, but it is like a part of me dying. She kept me from taking things too seriously.' Her look softened. "Chill out, Logan," she used to say.'

'As if you complemented each other.'

'Do you remember the Jesuit who used to keep repeating at days of recollection, "Let life question you"? I know now what he meant.'

In a natural gesture – but one that would have been forbidden in the days of de Chantal's convent formation – she reached out and held her friend's hand. 'Time, Deirdre,' she said, for want of a better word. 'Time heals all wounds.' They remained silent until one of the retired nuns strolled in for her afternoon tea; de Chantal released her grip. The old nun had been cleaning off dry stalks in the walled garden. 'Great to see the light in the sky again after the harsh winter we've had. God is very good to us, I always say.'

'Indeed He is.' De Chantal got up to fill the kettle.

The following Sunday afternoon, to escape from her own thoughts, Deirdre brought a batch of copybooks to the community room. There, beside one of the high windows that gave a splendid view of the Dublin hills, she settled down to correcting homework. The sun through the net curtains cast a tracery on the round table where she worked. At the television corner, Anselm was giving her cronies a blow-by-blow account of Gay Byrne's *The Late Late Show;* she went from that to *Coronation Street.*

Deirdre closed the copybooks and looked across at the three old nuns. They had forgotten the TV screen, where young people were having a great time in a piazza, taking photos and lazing in the sun while pigeons darted for scraps of food. The voiceover listed the sensational offers available in Italy for those who booked in time. Anselm was twisting her mouth in anger at Gay Byrne. He wasn't the worst of them, but he went too far at times, she thought. Like the night he had the lesbian nuns on. Anything to grab the headlines.

The walls were closing in: she had to get away or she would suffocate. She rushed through the remainder of the copies and hurried out as they were stirring themselves to go for a cup of tea and asking her to join them. After taking the long walk around by the lake, she made a visit to the cemetery. In the public park, across the valley, a man and a boy were playing a cup final. Shielding his eyes from the sun, the goalkeeper, in a mock-frenzied voice, gave a commentary while the boy placed the ball for a penalty – the last kick of the game. Liverpool had drawn even with Manchester United; now they had a chance to win the game.

She pushed open the gate and walked between rows of iron crosses. Shoots were already appearing on Ita's grave. She blessed herself, but whoops of delight from across the valley shattered her prayer: Michael Owen had scored for Liverpool. 'Come on, son,' the commentator called. 'Your ma will be looking for us.' Silence then, except for the voices from inside her head. And Ita's question: 'Is this it? Is this all there is?'

The names on the crosses tapped into a rich vein. Sister Mary Alphonsus had got first place at university but was forbidden to do further studies even after a letter from her professor pleaded for 'an exceptionally brilliant student'.

'I have prayed hard for your future,' Reverend Mother had told her, 'and I have decided that you will do the H Dip in September.' They needed a geography teacher in Fairview. Anyway, Reverend Mother didn't see the point of all these degrees: only turns a young Sister's head. And physics was fraught with danger. Scientists have no faith. The last Sister to do a doctorate left soon afterwards.

So Mary Alphonsus taught geography and religion and told everyone she was happy, and wore a paper hat every Christmas at the youth club, and joined in ring-a-ring-a-rosy. But when she reached the change of life she started polishing doorknobs. Very late one night another Sister found her in the refectory cleaning the cutlery. 'Getting rid of poisonous germs,' she whispered, and put a finger up to her mouth.

Deirdre shut the gate and took a last look at the serried rows of crosses. Perfect order even in death. She fixed her gaze on an empty stretch of ground by the ivy-covered wall on the far side until a cold breeze rushed through the laurel hedge, causing her to turn up the collar of her mackintosh and make hasten along the cypress-lined path to the daylight.

Over the years, she had grown used to the tiresome questions from examination classes: 'Why do we have to learn this Shakespeare?' and then, later, a more muted, 'What's going to come up in the exam, Sister Deirdre?'

'They're pathetic,' she used to complain to Ita. 'Education means nothing to them, only exam points. If it wasn't for a few in the Honours class, I'd go insane.' She got little sympathy. 'You're a Five, Logan. All Fives are intellectual snobs.'

But the classroom helped to calm the storm in her head about sickness and death and whether or not there's an afterlife. Towards the Easter holidays, she invited them back after school, or on Saturday mornings for tuition. Only the ambitious from the Honours class took up the offer. They moved the desks aside and sat around in a circle. Now, on the threshold of a grown-up world and wearing Russell Athletic instead of the plaid green wrap-over skirts, the pupils departed from the fixed routine and regarded their teacher as one of their own. The informal setting gave them courage to open up. 'Did Shakespeare believe in God, Sister Deirdre?'

'What's your own opinion?'

'You know where he says: "As flies to wanton boys we are to the Gods; they kill us for their sport".' An atheist since her father had died suddenly of a heart attack, Lee Anne, who was going to be a journalist, had a litany of angry questions.

'He also says: "There's a divinity that shapes our ends, roughhew them how we will".'

'Well, he didn't know about the laws of physics, as we do. And anyway, I don't believe in God. Certainly not an afterlife. When you die, that's the end.'

The word probed a nerve ending. As a nun, she ought to anchor the disparate comments; instead, she sat quietly while they got up steam about the death of God and religion. 'There's no hell. Definitely no hell.' They were at one on that issue. 'Heaven.' One girl shrugged her shoulders: 'Too good to be true,' she said. Her companion added: '"This life is not a rehearsal, so enjoy it while you can", my dad is always saying.' Inspired by Lee Anne, others expressed their atheism. Finally, Deirdre put aside *Hamlet*. 'There's no scientific proof, if that's what you want,' she said. 'More a matter of the heart.'

When she cleaned the blackboard, motes of chalk formed a beam of sunshine beside her desk: a slanted pillar from a roof light to the floorboards.

'Let me test your French.' She wrote: *'Le coeur a ses raisons que la raison ne connait point.'* They got it right after a couple of attempts.

'More a matter of the heart! Lee Anne was skeptical.

'That only means: if you're feeling good, if you're happy, then there's a God, because you want it to continue forever. Why does he allow whole families to be wiped out?'

They had forgotten Shakespeare, and Deirdre, who was listening to every word: the old questions about why we're here now taking on a new significance for her. They were so absorbed in the scandal of the Vatican's priceless art collection, and the way the Church looks down on women, that they lost track of time and she had to remind them about their bus.

Along with her teaching duties, she was a member of the Council: a representative body that met once a month with Sister Emmanuel, the Superior General, at the headquarters of the congregation in Terenure Road. This woman was near the end of her term in the top post. After three years of meetings and drafting position papers and vision statements, she had grown weary and was looking forward to Nigeria again, where she had been matron at Mary Immaculate Hospital.

Always willing to relieve her of administrative burdens, Sister Rita watched for an opening. At a previous meeting, she had volunteered to consult the agents about the land along Mill Road. Since becoming bursar, she had acquired knowledge of investments and had kept a close watch on the property section of the newspapers. She had negotiated the sale of convents in the country towns so well that she was given scope to carry out further investigation about Oak Hill, and had made a report back.

Though some hankered after the past, the nuns in the country towns accepted the inevitable and were appointed elsewhere; those that were no longer working returned to Belgrave, where they had begun as postulants. They had no alternative but to sell; a majority were on the verge of retirement and were unwilling to endure the headache of administering a school or a nursing home. At least they had the consolation of knowing that all other congregations were in the same boat.

The closure of the boarding school at Oak Hill was different. As far back as the turn of the century, past pupils had figured among the sprinkling of women at King's Inns. They could also be found among the sepia photos of consultants along the walls of St Vincent's and the Mater Hospital.

On this and every other matter, each nun had a right to express her views before a final vote was taken. And, deprived of a voice for years, they were determined to gain a hearing – on issues ranging from the colour of paint for the staircase to the arrangement of tables in the refectory. When the meetings dragged on, however, they began to grow weary of self-government. Some wished for the old days, when the Rule of Obedience spared them the tedium of endless debates about curtains and what procedures they should implement for booking the convent cars. Everything had suddenly grown complicated.

The Old Girls had a selection of snapshots, real or imagined, stored away in their hearts: sunny afternoons beneath the plane trees, the sound of balmy laughter when someone missed a shot at croquet and, in the distance, the heat-steam over the city. Deirdre too had her cameos. Waiting for the coach for Kingsbridge Station on her first Christmas holidays was unmixed joy. They chased each other around the suitcases at the front door. A young de Chantal, who calmed their night fears in the dormitory, now indulged their capers. In the icy air, their vaporised breath became cigarette smoke. 'Look, Sister de Chantal, I'm smoking.' Jack Frost glistened on the lawn, and a cloak of mist hung upon the lake.

On the advice of her Council, the Superior General called a meeting to decide the future of the boarding school. Rita delivered the main address and afterwards took questions from the floor. While some of the Old Girls voiced their regret, the vast majority offered no resistance. Before the speeches began, they had peered at the trends, forecasts and estimates posted on noticeboards at the top of the hall: another sign that the world they loved was slipping through their fingers. They had no choice except to float with the current.

For Rita, their silence was a blessed relief. If her own future hopes were to slot into place, she couldn't afford to raise anyone's hackles. During a break, she lingered with a few of the Old Girls.

'You handled the meeting very well,' one Old Girl told her.

'I can let you into a secret now.' She held her cup and saucer daintily in front of her face. 'I hardly slept a wink last night. The boarding school means so much to all of us.'

'You did great,' the others allowed. All this encouraged her to continue her homework on the sale of the land, which was worth around six million pounds, according to Mr Moloney. 'You'd be laughing all the way to the bank, Sister,' he said, like a teacher pointing out the obvious. 'With the Three Rock behind and a fine view of Dublin Bay – a crock of gold.'

He put on his reading glasses and surveyed the map. 'The arched gateway to Mill Road adds to the value. The young Celtic Tigers will feel they've it made when they drive through that every evening. There's a sucker born every minute, Sister!' The grin faded. 'Needs to be widened though.'

He turned the map around so that she could see for herself. After a few moments' reflection, she said: 'We have a problem.'

'What's that, Sister?'

'The old cemetery.'

'May I?' He took the map again.

'But our founder is buried there.'

'Yes. Well, of course. I see.' Not wanting to lose a hefty fee, he searched the map for a solution. 'Why not reinter, Sister? A colleague of mine was engaged in a similar project recently.' He held her eye for a moment.

She joined the auctioneer's search. Six million pounds was a lot of money. 'Leave it with me, Mr Moloney,' she said, after a little thought. 'I'll run it by the Council.' But before that, she would work behind the scenes, like she had when looking for grants from the Department of Education. 'Roast duck in the parlour and a hint that his children will have no bother getting a job in one of our schools – works wonders with inspectors,' a mentor had once whispered in her ear. And Rita was a fast learner.

A couple of evenings later, she began her campaign with Deirdre, who was washing cups in the kitchenette off the refectory. 'I'll dry,' she offered.

Nuns were leaving the refectory; others were still in clusters at the tables. 'The other day,' she said, 'I was thinking – it's been ages since Deirdre and myself have had a decent chat. How about a bite to eat? Lunch in Blake's some day?'

'That sounds OK.' But a bite to eat was never as simple as it seemed when the suggestion came from from Rita's lips.

'I was thinking of Saturday, if it would suit. We need to catch up.'

'That should be all right. I'll have to check the diary.'

After lunch on the Saturday, they drove up to Enniskerry; conversation skirted round the forthcoming Assembly. 'Hannah, to give her credit,' said Rita, 'has done Trojan work on getting a focus.'

'That's great.'

'We haven't had an Assembly now for three years. Can you believe it?'

Deirdre could. Sisters were no longer interested in making out position papers and mission statements to be consigned to the wastepaper basket or else to lie forgotten on some shelf with a mound of others.

They walked up the hill from the village. The wind changed: Rita talked about who was slowing up and who was the latest to be wheeled off to the nursing home. She was concerned. 'Only four out of seventeen are now salaried,' she noted. She was also worried about what to do with Belgrave. Some of the older nuns had opted to go back there rather than return to Oak Hill, the last stop before the grave.

'Slaney Mines would give anything for the house and grounds,' she said. 'It's not fair of the Old Girls, when they could come to us. Or go to the nursing home, where they'd have every creature comfort.'

At a junction, they took the road for the waterfall; Rita revealed who was applying for a sabbatical and who wanted to give up teaching to go into counselling: 'For your own ears only . . . ' she began. 'If you ask me, a lot of this counselling is only about getting control of people's lives.' She laughed when she recalled her own sabbatical in Spokane. 'All the group sessions and the self-analysis. I never saw the point of it. But I played the game. What's the use in digging up the past? My mother used always say, "You made your bed, now lie on it".'

While resting in the car after their walk, they flitted over more convent interests and watched a bus queue forming across from the obelisk; Rita fidgeted with her keys. 'There's something I'd like to run by you.' She told her about Moloney's proposal. 'I know it may sound rather mercenary, but that's not at all my objective. By no means. After all, most of the land has been lying idle for donkey's years. And all the orders are doing it now, anyway.'

Deirdre had a side view of the sharp profile behind the steering wheel. The penny dropped – the outing was a reconnaissance operation. 'Are we that badly off that we have to dig up the bones of these poor old nuns?'

'Yes. If you want to put it like that, yes. You have a point there.' Rita inserted the key. 'It would mean a much-needed injection of cash for our missionaries.'

Rita had no interest in the missions. When Sisters returned from Brazil reeling off the big guns of liberation theology – Boff and Gutiérrez – and demanding that they stop educating the well-off, she scoffed behind their backs. Her hands shot up, and she made inverted commas like rabbits' ears with her forefingers: '"Agents of the state" – so that's what the Third World groupies think of us. What next, I ask you?' On another occasion, she showed her hand: 'I'm keeping my head down until the "Third World"' – rabbits' ears again – 'get all this option for the poor out of their woolly combinations. That's for the Holy Rosarys and the Mercys; our work is to keep the home fires burning. Am I right?'

'Do we need so much to fund the missions? We've handed over Kenya and Chile and all we've left is Nigeria and the Sudan.'

'Yes, but the salaries are getting fewer.' The last thing Rita wanted was to draw swords before the battle began. She started tapping the steering wheel, and, as they were driving through Stepaside, pointed to the city. 'Fabulous view, isn't it?'

At an early age, she had picked up the fear of poverty. 'Keep an eye on him, like a good girl,' her mother used to say, while she stuffed banknotes down the front of her blouse; outside the shop window, her father had talked about greyhounds and great footballers of yore to his cronies.

The ritual was followed by a bus trip to the Munster and Leinster Bank in Naas. Coming home, she had learned about Shelbourne Park and Cheltenham – and other such places where foolish men squander their money and leave their families badly off. But despite her mother's vigilance, they ended up in Marian Terrace, of all places, with some of the ne'er-do-wells of the town. From then on, Rita spent every evening around at the convent on Castle Street. The nuns liked her and gave her little jobs: arranging flowers in the parish church or going to the shops for odds and ends. And they allowed her to attend, free of charge, piano lessons and Irish dancing classes for which the doctor's daughters and others had to pay tuition fees.

She also lobbied other nuns. 'After all, this is now an everyday thing where congregations are putting property to good use. And then we have the upkeep of Mary Immaculate. CAT scans and hospital equipment don't fall off the trees.'

Hannah felt they should go for it. The Brothers in Temple-ogue had to do the same – for the good of the order. 'Count on my support,' she told Rita, 'but right now I'm up to my eyes at the retreat centre.'

At a council meeting they put the final touches to the Easter Assembly. Hannah would lead them in a discernment exercise she had learned at Berkeley. They would also have to set the ball rolling for the hundred-and-twenty-fifth anniversary of the foundation, the Superior General said: 'Only two years away, and God alone knows who'll be left – if anyone – in twenty-five years' time.' Hannah proposed a mission statement for the new millennium. Bríd looked across at Deirdre and threw her eyes to heaven. They had spent months rejigging the last one when the fall in numbers caused them to release their grip on schools and hospitals.

The mission statement out of the way, Rita put them in the picture about the auctioneer's evaluation of the land, without mentioning the cemetery. 'They would welcome some of that at Mary Immaculate, now that they're on an expansion programme,' she said for the Superior General, who came to life at the mention of her old stamping ground.

At Emmanuel's election, the returned missionaries and the old Oak Hill girls had been at loggerheads about who would hold the balance of power. Caught up in a fever of working for the 'marginalized', the Third World wanted to give away land for halting sites, stop educating the well-off and live a simple life. Some of them had gone to live on corporation estates, setting themselves a budget in line with social-welfare allowances. Bríd gave up after six weeks. 'I've no intention of living on mouldy cheese and in a freezing house at this stage of my life,' she said. 'I never went in much for masochism, anyway,' she told someone. Gradually the fever subsided. Some returned to the missions; others left.

Sister Emmanuel had been a compromise to satisfy both lobbies. As matron of Mary Immaculate in Lagos, she did a twelve-hour shift and was lucky if she got a few days during Christmas to rest in a convent up the coast, where she had a few friends. After her day's work, she was often called out in the thick darkness to deliver a baby. Behind her in the hut, the father held a lantern, only the whites of his eyes showing in the shadow. This had been her schedule for sixteen years but, as she often reflected, it was real work – not sitting around a table devising mission statements.

While the rest were on their way out the door after the meeting, she called Deirdre aside in the front hall. 'We'll have privacy in here,' she said, leading the way to a side parlour. 'I've asked Rita to hold on; she's waiting in the kitchen with Hannah.'

With her back to the window, she put Deirdre in mind of a comment from a nun who had worked with her in Africa. 'Emmanuel is sound, but I'd prefer to be with her than against her. And behind those glasses, you wouldn't know whether she's looking at you or not.'

'We should all get together more often, Deirdre,' she was now saying. She hoped the numbers would be up from the last Assembly. 'Especially some of the people who have been most vocal about inclusiveness.' They chatted on, both knowing it was a warm-up exercise. Then the Superior General stole a glance at her watch and got down to business.

'I'm anxious to have a biography done on Catherine for the anniversary,' she said. Our founder's life has never been given proper treatment. We have *A Light in the Window* by Jerome, God be good to her, but that was written thirty years ago.' Then she stopped. 'There's a lot of material that shows Catherine to be way ahead of her time. Someone we can be proud of. Her work for social justice has never been written up. Did you know she was a great letter-writer to the papers?'

'Never knew that.'

'We were told very little about her. A pity, because she could have an appeal for anyone thinking of joining. That's if we ever get anyone again.' She looked directly at Deirdre. 'I'd like you to do it.'

'A biography?'

'I know you've had a lot on your plate in the past few months, going in to St Vincent's, and then Ita's death, God rest her, but you could take your time. And I'd get someone to relieve you of your teaching duties.' She wanted one of their own to do the book, and she had implicit trust in Deirdre. God alone knows what an outsider might do with the material, she thought. Rummaging through files in her office, she had come upon a memo left by a predecessor: 'Treat *sub secreto* all archival documents and records dealing with our founder.'

'It's not everyone you can open the family closet to,' she said.

'I've no experience of writing the likes of a biography,' Deidre commented.

'A first in English? None of us is more qualified.' She would give her all the help she needed. 'Don't decide now.'

Sister Emmanuel shifted in the chair in a way that suggested the interview was coming to an end. 'I'll get Rita to give you the keys of the archives and you can see for yourself. Whatever you decide, Deirdre, I'll understand.'

That weekend Rita took her to the archives, now kept in the Red House, a two-storey Georgian building that stood across the lawn from the convent. Over the years it had become known as Catherine's Retreat. The handed-down version held that she used spend a couple of days there after returning from a sea journey, to rest and to escape the constant stream of callers. In Deirdre's schooldays the house was where Mother General and her assistants lived.

When Rita unlocked one of the doors off the spacious front hall, the smell of old books and papers rose to meet them. Stacks of files filled the metal shelves. In a glass cabinet was a ballgown of white corded silk with a plain bodice; in another, a riding crop and hat. She indicated with her keys: 'That's the dress she was wearing the night of the Shelbourne Ball.' As novices, they had all been given the standard account of Catherine's call to help the poor.

'Herself wants them all out of here and put on show for the celebrations.' Rita's comments ebbed and flowed while Deirdre looked around.

In her room that evening, she found herself mulling over the riding crop and the young woman who rode to hounds. She went down to the Long Parlour and took a closer look at her portrait. 'That was done at Sackville Park, her father's estate in County Meath, soon after she returned from finishing school in Paris,' one of the nuns had once told her. The creases that had later lined her face from battling with bishops were absent here; instead, a determined woman looked out at the world, one hand resting on a grand piano.

Apart from the time she spent as Principal at Oak Hill, Deirdre had been over twenty-two years in the classroom: she was due a sabbatical. Her friends had been urging her to go to one of the American centres for renewal such as Berkeley or Spokane, but she had no great desire to return 'owning my feelings', or with a West Coast glossary. And anyway, her students' results every August had become a stimulant to do even better the following year.

Lately, however, the classroom challenge was beginning to slacken; this she put down to the tiredness that affects every teacher of her age. At odd moments her thoughts kept returning to that determined face and the Great House world of Sackville Park. Her curiosity about the founder was growing: Catherine must have been more than the plaster saint she, as a postulant, had received from the novice mistress.

The Superior General wrote from Rome as soon as Deirdre agreed to do the biography. Her ability was a great blessing for the congregation, the letter said. They would meet, on her return. Rita also received a note, and called to her room one morning with a set of keys for the archives and for an adjoining office, equipped with a computer and a telephone: 'And anything else you want. Thanks a mill'.' She winked and was gone out the door, leaving a draught of perfumed soap. The other rooms in the Red House were used for meetings. A couple of nuns back from São Paulo had set up what they called a Justice Desk. They were forever heaving black plastic bags up and down the steps.

On a low table near the electric fire was a copy of the centenary book, with, next to the flyleaf, a letter from the Vatican:

Segreteria Di Stato

Vatican City

May 5, 1973

On the occasion of the Centenary of the Canonical
Erection of the Congregation of the Precious Blood,
the Holy Father cordially imparts to the Reverend
Mother General and Religious Community, in
pledge of abiding divine assistance, His Apostolic
Blessing.

A. G. Cardinal Cicognani

She sat and leafed through black-and-white photos: girls in the
uniform of bygone years played hockey in a stagy way for the
camera. Further on were a group of nuns in wimple and gimp at
the steps of a TWA plane. The caption read: 'Precious Blood Sisters
arriving at Idlewild 16 August 1951 – the year we opened St
Charles Borromeo High School in Holyoak.' On another page
was a photo of herself – the one they used for promoting vocations
– with the heading: 'Would you like to devote your life to God?'
Her first Leaving Certificate class at Mespil Road. On the
blackboard her handwriting: ''Tis the infirmity of his age, he hath
but ever slenderly known himself.' Lear: the foolish old man who
had to learn the hard way.

She resolved to steer clear of the Red House until after the
examinations, but like a child who makes for a new toy first thing
in the morning, she found herself drawn to the prayer books and
papers, some of them so brittle she had to lay them out on the
desk. Spiritual reflections in Latin and French were recorded in
the founder's own writing. In a shoebox was a Catholic Truth

Society booklet on her life: *From the Drawing Room to the Cloister*, published in 1948 by Burns and Oates. She scanned the pages. The final paragraphs traced the spread of Precious Blood Sisters in Ireland, North America, Africa and New Zealand. Letters of praise from bishops echoed each other. She read the one from California, where she had taught for a few years:

> We have come to know the deep faith and un-swerving loyalty of the Sisters, and have come to admire their dedication to the education of children.
>
> We acknowledge the precious gifts, the treasures for enriching Catholic education in the excellence of the religious life of Precious Blood Sisters. We think of them, their prayer, skill, devotedness, culture and grace as a great blessing from God to mankind.
>
> Sincerely Yours in Christ,
> + James, Cardinal Archbishop of Los Angeles

The booklet made a passing reference to her 'difference of opinion' with Bishop Gibbons of Limerick and Archbishop Talbot of Dublin, but the account was so full of sweetness and light it bore little resemblance to the events that took place.

One chapter contained the standard version every postulant received during her first days in the convent. Catherine Browne was the only daughter of a land-owning family in County Meath who could trace their line back to the twelfth century. They were connected to some of the great Anglo-Irish families, such as the Butlers and the Ormonds. An uncle had fled to France after a duel and had become a general in Napoleon's army.

The book gave a glowing description of Catherine's calling, and how poor Mr De Lacy was broken-hearted when she called off their engagement. But her family gave her every support in her courageous decision. On visiting days, novices loved telling this to their relatives in the parlours, especially the Shelbourne Ball episode. They were so proud of her decision to give up such a high place in society to do the Lord's work. The true story bore little resemblance to that simple account.

*

That night outside the Shelbourne, Catherine and her fiancé, Henry De Lacy, and another couple, Mr Basil Crawford and his lady friend, were returning from the opening ball of the season. It was a sultry night, cherry blossoms lay scattered on the footpath at the corner of St Stephen's Green, when the two ladies linked their escorts on the way to their carriage. While the driver was waiting in line for broughams and other carriages to move off, Catherine took in the brilliant spectacle. The music floated out through the open windows of the hotel: the orchestra was playing a final Strauss waltz. Gentlemen in white scarves and their lady friends were pouring out of the main door, talking in an excited way, and outdoing each other as they recalled incidents from the night. Bursts of laughter enriched the jollity. Mr Crawford's lady friend, who had a weakness for uniforms, pointed out in an excited way the red coats and gold epaulettes of the Guards, and the black corded jackets of the Rifles.

But Catherine's attention was elsewhere. A bunch of ragged children had taken shape out of the dark lanes of Irishtown and Ringsend and were sidling along by the railings to get a closer look and maybe a coin from the quality. She tried to gain Mr De Lacy's attention, but he paid her no heed.

'My word, the season has begun in splendid fashion,' Mr Crawford was saying. He tapped the glass with his cane. 'I say, driver, are we to remain here for the rest of our lives.' They laughed. Mr Crawford was awfully amusing. 'Driver, look lively,' he repeated, and struck the floor.

The chatter ceased when they saw Catherine, without a word to anyone, rise from her seat and leave the carriage. Bemused, they looked after her as she walked towards the huddle, took a coin from her purse and held it out to the leader. The girl – taller than the rest – stared at her for a moment, grabbed the money and swept the others to the nearest side street so that they looked like some grotesque body with many legs being swallowed up by the darkness.

Catherine slept badly that night. At breakfast her father, Richard Browne, at his townhouse to see a member of parliament, had a string of questions put to him. For a while he indulged his daughter's attack on social injustice and wished that his sons would show some of her spirit instead of cavorting around London. But his mood changed while listening to the tirade. He should have anticipated this in her character: even as a child she was rather strange, preferring to read than play with dolls. Then there was her reluctance to be presented with other debutantes at the Castle Drawing Room. 'Lining up with those whose deepest thought is to gain a husband, I find decidedly odious,' she had answered back when the letter of invitation arrived from the Lord Lieutenant.

Now she was wearying him with the social reforms of Charles Kingsley and someone called Engels. Did either of these men ever do a decent day's work apart from filling people's heads with impractical notions, he wondered, while she continued with her attack. If they were working themselves to the bone and providing jobs they would have less time for spreading propaganda. He had enough on his mind: his distilleries at Cavan and Athlone had survived that troublesome friar, Father Matthew, and his confounded temperance campaign. Now a government decision to encourage beer drinking had put a dent in his trade.

He waved away a servant holding a teapot at his side. 'My dear, your foolhardiness in leaving the carriage distresses me. You could have been set upon. Those ragamuffins are often decoys for robbers. You could also have imperilled the welfare of your companions.' He regarded her plump face. When she is married and with children, she'll forget all this Kingsley and social-reform nonsense, he thought to himself.

*

Deirdre sat at her desk and looked out a back window at a row of single-storey houses that were once the stables for Oak Hill – De Valera's Townhouse, they called them when she was a boarder. She'd heard the story so often: Matilda had given him refuge during the War of Independence. As a novice, she had served tea when he arrived for his annual visit the week before Christmas and had listened as the old nuns fawned on the blind President. He repeated the same litany of praises about the Precious Blood Sisters and how happy he had been during his short term as a teacher there.

She was finding herself drawn to this woman who had turned her back on privilege, and was beginning to glimpse a real person behind the milk-and-water version. Like other novices, she had inherited the well-worn stories about the founder: how she had never intended setting up a religious congregation, nor intended that the Precious Blood Congregation would ever be subject to a bishop's jurisdiction. But Deirdre was too busy being a nun to pay too much heed to the small print.

Doubts, on the other hand, began to grow about spending a year or two plodding through documents and staring at a computer screen. For what? A few hundred would be sold; each convent in Ireland would buy one for the community room, or the library. Nuns on the missions would dip in during an idle moment, and then it would lie on some coffee table, the jacket fading in the tropical sun.

Since her boarding-school days, she had been familiar with the gilt-edged picture of the founder in the library. She opened the centenary book and examined a photocopy, but one side of her face was hidden by a shadow.

Idle conversation during holidays at Tramore came to life again in her head. De Chantal and her cronies swapping anecdotes to brighten a misty afternoon while they sat in the glass porch overlooking the strand. Catherine wanted to be a man when she was a child, one of them claimed: 'Yes, she announced that she would take over her father's estate – it had become a family joke.'

De Chantal held court on these occasions. After a gin and tonic, she was in her seventh heaven, especially with a captive audience. The anecdotes came tumbling out – like the day she had them in stitches about nuns in the nineteenth century, and how they didn't wear any knickers.

'Has work commenced?' she asked Deirdre one day while she was weeding the rose garden in front of the Red House.

'As soon as the exams are over next week, I'll get cracking.'

'Don't make her out to be a plaster saint. We've had enough of that.'

'I'm only browsing, de Chantal.' Deirdre shaded her eyes as she looked across the lawn at the copper beeches. 'The evening outside the Shelbourne seems to have been a watershed, but I've a sense there's more to that woman's life than meets the eye.'

'Window dressing.' De Chantal's dark eyes lit up. 'When

Jerome was doing the booklet for the centenary, I gave her a bit of help with proof-reading and cataloguing documents.' With one hand at the small of her back, she raised herself. 'If you want to find the real Catherine, take a look in the safe. Her diaries. I put them back in the drawer, but that was nearly thirty years ago. It's a risk, of course, and I wouldn't like to see you hurt.'

'There's another Catherine in the diaries?'

'There's always another story to tell. The one hidden beneath the hagiography.' De Chantal removed her gardening gloves and gathered up the tools. 'You might never use them, but at least you'll meet a real person. There are journals also, minutes of meetings – I doubt if they've ever seen the light of day before or since. Struggles she had with bishops until she went straight to the Pope. More than we were ever told.'

'Very unusual to do something like that. Diaries were for public consumption in those days.'

'Catherine was an unusual woman. Who knows, maybe she wanted the truth to be known. Anyway, why does Emmanuel want a biography done?'

'She feels that Catherine could have great appeal for today's world. You know – women's independence, and the way she fought for the rights of the poor.'

A rueful smile spread across de Chantal's face. 'She might get more than she bargained for.'

'How do you mean?'

Another sister came trudging towards them with a watering can, so de Chantal lowered her voice: 'If you want to write something more than a pious account, take a look in the safe. *Bí cúramach.*'

Deirdre was anxious to see the diaries, but she had to meet her students after the exams: go over the questions, congratulate some and console others. Like other years, the results, when they came out in August, would be among the best in Dublin: proof positive for parents that their faith in Precious Blood schools, especially Oak Hill, was well grounded.

She had other chores to look after too. The number of drivers was decreasing, so she was often called on to chauffeur a sister to the train station or the dentist. Once a month she took Joan and one or two others to Dr Harrington, a psychiatrist in Fitzwilliam Square.

From time to time, she journeyed down the glass corridor to the nursing home with sisters who could no longer ward off the fateful moment. They were always forgetting things, and wanting to go back to collect bits and pieces: hankies, a comb or a brush, cough sweets. Then other little items they would never use but which they hoarded like magpies in their bedside locker: spools of thread, buttons, patches and safety pins; for no obvious reason, that saddened her. To avoid the same journey for as long as possible, their contemporaries tagged along with the Vincent de Paul or the Legion of Mary. De Chantal played bridge, went for a massage once a week and gave grinds in French and Irish. 'Anything,' as she said herself, 'but the cannery.' Anselm supervised food supplies and gleaned every scrap of gossip from the women who worked in the kitchen. At Nutgrove Shopping Centre, she learned from the sergeant's wife about the night Bríd and the Tallaght curate were found out.

One of the old nuns had noticed a strange car parked down by the lake, and when it was still there at bedtime she telephoned the guards. At lunch that day Bríd had been excited: she was going to a Colour-Me-Beautiful night, and for a pizza afterwards, she told them, 'with a few of the girls.'

Aidan Doyle had begun to call since the funeral. On Deirdre's birthday, he arrived with a bottle of Nina Ricci; another time he brought her a duty-free scarf; nevertheless, each time she managed to steer him to the refectory. Before he got into his car one day, he looked at her over the roof of it. 'What does a fellow have to do to talk to you alone?' he asked. 'No chance of coming out for a meal?'

She gave in eventually. 'I'm glad we met up again,' he told her when they were seated in Roly's. She looked across, but he was studying the menu. A boy in reading glasses: happy so long as his appetites were satisfied. That story Anselm told – no doubt for her benefit – was probably true: how he and his widow friend had been seen strolling along the seafront at Bray. Yet he was a link with the past, and for some strange reason, against all common sense, she felt drawn to him.

The Superior General and her Council decided to confine the Assembly to the Whit weekend so that those who were teaching would be able to attend. Less than half the congregation, however, turned up. Many of those who lived in the country had free transport and were delighted with the prospect of a train journey.

On the Friday evening, they came together at Oak Hill. 'We will review our partnership in mission,' Rita said after the Superior General had given the opening address, 'and journey together to discern where our energies should be invested.' Hannah would take them through a process of reflection. 'We have spent good money on her education in Berkeley,' she quipped. 'Now is the time to see if it has been put to good use.'

Feet planted far apart on the floor, Hannah stood beside an overhead projector. She dismissed any suggestions of having a head start on anyone or that she would be giving a lecture. Instead, 'You will be doing the work,' she said, grinning. They muttered a playful protest.

'To initiate a process of sharing,' she said, one hand resting on a sturdy hip, 'we will brainstorm in clusters so that we can discern the issues before us.' She placed a sheet of acetate on the projector. 'Sisters, all of these help us to indicate whether we are in the zone of God's will.' Like a schoolteacher, she ran a ruler along the different topics. 'So let's brainstorm.'

The younger nuns had been used to brainstorming at teachers' meetings and self-development courses. The others were lost. And, instead of keeping to the group discussion, they reverted to unfinished topics from the breakfast table: how honey and vinegar taken first thing in the morning could cure arthritis, how young people never show respect for their superiors, and how to play computerised Solitaire.

One of the Old Girls, a joker, raised her hand like a student in an examination hall. 'Hannah,' she called. The others stopped brainstorming and looked towards her. She read out one of the exercises. '"Am I experiencing anger, resentment, desolation or desire?" With the greatest respect, I have no intention of sharing any of the first three except with my confessor. And as for the last' – she paused – 'if it means what I think it means – what we used call carnal desire – the next time I feel such a rush coming on, I'll sing a *Te Deum*.'

Her hair fresh from the shower, Bríd arrived during the break.

She rested her mobile on one of the tables and sipped her coffee. 'A present from my niece for my silver jubilee,' she explained to a couple of nuns from Fermoy who were talking to Anselm. No sooner had she turned her back than Anselm clutched the handbag she took with her everywhere, and gave her cronies the lowdown. 'Pillow talk with the boyfriend – a long time, though, since he was a boy.' She pursed her thin lips. 'That's what she uses it for. You could hear her giggling between the sheets, I'm told.'

They assembled for a short input from Hannah. Again they would brainstorm for twenty minutes. She ran the ruler along another acetate: 'How we can spend quality time with each other and yet find space for ourselves.' They would take a look at the role of women religious and 'the anger we feel at the institutional church'. Zoe, also a Precious Blood Sister from Rhode Island, took over. Taking turns, the two of them conducted the session. They had met at Berkeley and, when the Providence community closed down, Zoe had asked for a transfer to Ireland. Nearly every day they phoned each other, and at least once a week Zoe came to Oak Hill for her tea. 'We are blessed to have Zoe, who is a highly qualified group therapist.' said Hannah, and led the applause.

'Sisters,' said the American nun, 'we need to do some spring-cleaning. Anger at the male-dominated church can drain our zip.' In a pinstriped trousers suit and loafers, she strode back and forth while she questioned whether they should expend their vigour on a rotten system, even though they ought to expunge those hurts from the past. Suddenly, the afternoon yawning stopped. Instead of brainstorming, they asked for a plenary session. The facilitator was pleased; she kicked off with, 'Sisters, we are tired of being second-class citizens in the church. Some of us are licking envelopes for pastors when we should be gainfully employed.'

'Employed, Sister? That's a joke.' A nun with a pudding-bowl hairstyle stood up. 'More like slave labour.' She was proud to be among a gathering of emancipated women who knew their own minds and would no longer bend the knee to male authority figures. She was running women's groups in Galway and the future most definitely belonged to them. 'Very soon not many will be going to Mass. Priests will be as dead as the dodo.' That got a laugh.

Thinly veiled anger about past hurts flared up. They recounted the many times they had trotted off to the kitchen after Mass to serve the chaplain's breakfast in the parlour.

'Do you remember,' said a nun, ' when we had to whip off the apron and sleeves when the bell rang.'

'For the fifth or sixth time in one day,' added another, 'when priests on holidays came to say Mass.'

'Rent-a-congregation,' Hannah sneered. A sister from Athlone stood up. At forty-seven, she had decided she wasn't going to be tied to a classroom until retirement age, so she was now working with a retreat team. They shouldn't get bogged down in what was now an old curiosity shop: 'I'm heavily invested in helping people find space for God and not wasting time on priests.' Her supporters chuckled. 'I now find my work gives me great energy.' For a while, 'energy' became a catchword. The younger nuns latched on, and shared the joys of newly found interests – from aromatherapy to healing with herbs.

'Let's continue to live the gospel of love, Sisters,' was Zoe's final comment, 'but let it be tough love.'

After supper a working group presented a draft of the mission statement. This they would consider over the following months, before a final polish. Towards nightfall, an old nun put up her hand. 'Excuse me, Mary Placidus – I mean, Hannah – what time is Mass in the morning?'

'Morning Prayer and Communion is at eight, Josephine.'

'But Mass – we're not Protestants. What time is Mass?'

'We have prepared a liturgy with inclusive language that I think will mean a lot to all of us. Have a look at the handout. But I know where you're coming from, Josephine.'

'What's she saying?' For a moment she was put off and fumbled with the controls of her hearing aid. 'Coming from? In the name of God!' She appealed to her companions, who urged her on. 'Doesn't she know I'm coming from Fethard. Do you mean there's no Mass? Where's the chaplain? And shouldn't we have a priest here now to guide us. That nice little Jesuit from Manresa that we had for the summer retreat.'

The old nun picked up a copy of the Order of Service and read the Lord's Prayer according to Zoe: '"Our Father and Mother who art in heaven, hallowed be thy name." What religion is this? Have we all lost whatever screed of sense we have?'

A murmur of irritation came from her supporters, and one or two stood to speak, but Rita intervened. A block vote against the real business the following day would ruin her plan. 'Yes, of course we will have Mass in the chapel. We thought you might like the option of a lie-in.'

'Option? Option about Mass? What's the world coming to?'

'The chaplain will be here for Mass at seven thirty, Josephine,' Rita reassured her.

Hannah, named 'Primrose' by one of her sixth classes because of her sullen looks, turned her rear end to the gathering and picked up her stencils. The pre-Berkeley pout made a brief reappearance. She hit the switch of the projector as others were streaming out, offering her compliments.

They had drinks in the community room that night. In one corner was a table with bottles of gin, bacardi, wine and Bally-gowan. The small talk was anecdotal, and meant to defuse the vestiges of tension after the day's work. One incident primed another. Nuns long dead were recalled and depicted as high-principled and dedicated. Generous to a fault.

One sister contributed an account of her departure for a new mission in Providence, Rhode Island, in 1962. Six of them boarded the *Rotterdam* at Cobh; they played cards and went to movies every day, and the captain called them 'My five insurance angels.' He invited them for dinner on the last night before they docked at New York.

'I went soon afterwards,' Anselm declared, 'in the *US America*. It was heavenly. We met a group of young priests in their suits and Roman collars. We were on deck one day and one poor priest's hat was blown overboard. The others joked that he wouldn't need a hat where he was going. That it never rains in Los Angeles.'

'Priests in those days knew how to dress, not like today's crop,' said a nun beside her.

'In Providence,' Anselm continued, 'we all had to pitch in. For my sins, I was made Reverend Mother.'

After her second gin and tonic, Bríd was listening in a cloudy silence. Bitter memories were winging their way back from Providence. A local priest used to visit her classroom: during a heatwave he brought her an electric fan. One day while she was keeping an eye on the children, he accompanied her around the playground; both were unaware of Anselm's black looks through her office window. 'I told you before about talking to that priest,' she snapped, when they were alone in the lunchroom. 'Now go straight to bed. I'll take over your class. You'd be well advised to reconsider your vocation, or some other congregation might take you, if they're that foolish.' Sending them to bed in the daytime was Anselm's favourite punishment.

'I suppose, God forgive me, I made many a blunder,' she was now saying.

'Ah, you did your best,' they chorused.

'Yes, indeed. You did fine.'

'Times were different.'

'You were a bitch, Anselm.' Bríd's words sliced the air. The others gawped at her. She laughed and took another sip. They attempted a chuckle, but she launched into another blitz. 'The way you made servants of us, bringing up your glass of milk and biscuit, and turning back the bedclothes for Your Ladyship.'

Anselm's mouth began to turn and twist – once a signal to put the fear of God into a novice. But her power to bully had long been spent. 'Yes, I suppose I did many wrong things,' she conceded. 'But, sure, that's water under the bridge.'

'The scars remain, Anselm.'

One of the nuns put on a broad smile: 'Now, isn't all this great that we're together again? What time did Rita say we'll begin in the morning?'

Apart from Brid, they all responded to the convent way of whitewashing, and returned to safe topics. Hannah's exercises on sharing were great, weren't they? She had gained so much from her time in America. 'Yes, Hannah has her feet on the ground.'

No sooner had Brid picked up her mobile and left, than they turned to console Anselm, who was now sobbing into her handkerchief. 'It's not the time nor the place,' she cried. 'I was only doing what was my duty.'

'Of course, Anselm, don't mind her,' they said. 'Bríd doesn't know half the time what she's saying.'

Later on, Bríd met Deirdre in the ground corridor. Still seething, she recounted the run-in: 'My blood boils when I think of the way they tried to put us down.' They could hear the crunch of gravel outside the Gothic windows and the murmur of conversations as the other Sisters strolled up and down the ambulatory. Bríd needed a breath of fresh air to clear her headache.

'If I was twenty years younger, I'd be gone in the morning.' The floodlighting cast an amber glow on the granite arches. 'I look after number one, Deirdre. Do my job and try to keep my sanity. We were slaveys for too long.' She pulled her cardigan around her shoulders. 'They go on about the male-dominated church, but they're no better themselves when they have a bit of power. And Emmanuel – though she means well – I remember nurses telling me, when she was Matron in Athlone, she used to poke them in the ribs in the morning to see that they had a full slip on.'

'She wouldn't get away with it now,' Deirdre added. 'We were always told she ran Mary Immaculate like a sewing machine.'

Bríd calmed down. 'Talking about slaveys, do you remember O'Connell Street?'

'Could I ever forget.'

It was their name for the Long Corridor. The Ritz, they called the set of toilets at one end. As novices, they did their turn on O'Connell Street and the Ritz, scrubbing the tiles from one staircase to the other. She remembered the rattle of aluminium buckets afterwards in the sluice room, and the squelch of mops when they squeezed the heads in the draining trough. The smell of Dettol had hung in the air, and remained on their hands when they went to the chapel.

Her anger now spent, Bríd began to regret her outburst. 'I don't know what comes over me. That Anselm. I know, I know,' – she was chopping the air with her hand – 'I shouldn't let her get to me. And she wasn't all that bad. You remember when we were boarders and she was in charge of the infirmary?'

'Calling every night to see were we all right?'

'What happens to us?'

'Too long a sacrifice.'

'I'll not be drawn the next time.' They were quiet for a moment, then Bríd began to chuckle to herself. 'What in God's name has she in the handbag that she has to guard it with her life?'

'They used to say when she was Bursar that she carried around the convent funds.'

'More like the crown jewels.'

Deirdre had had enough talk of Anselm. 'What did you think of today's proceedings?'

'A waste of paper. What ever becomes of these assemblies? A smokescreen. The main picture is tomorrow. No one reads these reports or vision statements.' The tap of high heels filled the cloister with a hollow sound.

'What would really make you sick are the speeches about the old sisters. How was it Rita put it? "Be assured that we have a high estimate of your experience and expertise." Only last week, she told me to make sure Berchmans is never let near the key of the drinks cabinet. And that poor old creature likes nothing better than a sherry at night.'

Rita, Hannah and Zoe passed by. 'There go the champions of quality time,' said Bríd under her breath. 'They love the community so much they disappear to Blake's for lunch. You're the last of the romantics if you believe any of this.'

Deirdre didn't.

'Yesterday,' Rita began, after Sister Emmanuel had given a short opening address, 'we had a really good sharing. Today we will put our sense of support for each other into practice.' She spoke about Jesus' love for the poor and how Catherine Browne had received her inspiration from witnessing the wretched conditions of Dublin's street children.

'Precious Blood Sisters have always been faithful to that objective, as well as responding to the educational needs of girls from good Catholic homes. Many have happy memories of their boarding-school days; past pupils of Oak Hill, no matter what part of the world they find themselves in, remain loyal to their alma mater.'

The sales pitch was for the Old Girls. She needn't have bothered. They accepted that it had to close; the few muted comments that came from the floor related to the safety of the stained-glass window to St Francis, and that it wouldn't end up in some pub.

'Oh, that will be taken care of,' Rita assured her. 'I'm very glad to let you know that it will find a good home. A parish priest in Kildare wants it for a new church.'

They were pleased. 'And what about the photographs along the ground-floor corridor?' asked an Old Girl.

'They will be stored safely and hung here in the convent.'

'Thank God.' The Old Girl sat down.

Sister Emmanuel expressed her regret that a shortage of vocations had forced this decision upon them, but felt certain 'that

Catherine up in heaven is nodding in agreement this morning.'

Two Sisters working in the Sudan gave a report on tribal warfare, starvation and disease: they needed money to run their medical centres and schools. Returned missionaries who were living in corporation houses led the tide of sympathy: during Ronald Reagan's visit they had carried placards outside the US Embassy. Closure of the boarding school was long overdue, they said, and they made bold proposals for helping the missions and the parishes where sisters were making 'an option for the poor'. The Old Girls joined the flow: 'Cake sales or one of these Christmas fasts – good training for our pupils to know what these unfortunates suffer.' This angered the missionaries: pennies for the black babies and miteboxes went out with the Ark.

But the Superior General intervened: 'Any help, no matter how small, is appreciated in the missions, but we'll have to devote more – much more – now that we are selling off valuable property.' After a coffee break, they would decide on an issue far more significant than the closure of the boarding school, she said. 'But we have to balance good management and the right use of property with principles of integrity. We cannot sell our souls for a mess of pottage.'

Rita fidgeted with her chain. The Superior's cautious tone might tip the scales against her plan. Already the proposal was receiving a mixed reaction when they whispered about it in the refectory or while watching TV. During the break, she collogued with Hannah. 'They might be damn thankful when they're shuffling down the corridor to the nursing home. Money for round-the-clock nursing and chemists' bills doesn't fall off the trees.' She had a ready smile and a word of greeting for passers-by. 'And I've no intention,' she said through her teeth, 'of ending my days in the open ward of a public hospital, waking every morning to the stench of incontinence.'

After lunch the gloves came off. 'Making space' and 'spending quality time' evaporated like mist in a heatwave. Rita defended her proposal. 'Several religious orders have done this, and it's always done with the greatest respect for the dead. The ceremony of reinterment is carried out with dignity. Officials from the corporation and a priest are always present.' But all the old nuns could see was an iron shovel plunging into the bones of their predecessors. One or two began to cry when their arguments failed.

'Is this going to be another Enniskerry?' asked a nun whose ancestor had accompanied Catherine Brown on the first mission to Nigeria.

The Enniskerry episode had made banner headlines. A garage owner in the village who had heard that the nuns were selling out lock, stock and barrel made them an offer, well above the market value, but only if they were willing to move the cemetery. While filling the kettle one morning, the curate there looked out his kitchen window, and was astounded by the mounds of fresh earth in the convent cemetery. Thinking the worst, he rang the guards. The sergeant calmed his fears about body-snatching: 'You must be a sound sleeper, Father.' He laughed as he gave the details.

During the night the Sisters had arranged for the remains to be exhumed and to be taken to the Mother House cemetery. With powerful lights, and screens around the graves, they had supervised the dig-up by men with shovels and a JCB. An official from the county council was there to see that they had twenty-four skulls to correspond to the same number of death certificates. They were supposed to provide a coffin for each remains, but someone said afterwards that the bones were gathered up and filled into half that number.

'I want to reassure you,' said one of Rita's supporters, 'experts in this work will carry out the exhumation in a dignified way – and in broad daylight. They use brushes and special tools – like they do in archaeological sites – so have no fears on that score.'

Hannah switched on the projector and an upside-down map appeared on the wall. 'As you can see,' she said, straightening the architect's survey plan, 'we are not interfering with the aesthetics of Oak Hill. Look: the lake, the grove and the playing areas remain ours. Good thing the classrooms are in another building so we can knock the dormitories to make room for parking and a separate entrance.'

'What about a preservation order?' an Old Girl asked.

Rita intervened: 'We're lucky, there's no preservation order on that portion.'

'Knock everything for money,' muttered the nun, who had enquired about Mass times.

Rita ignored her. 'We owe it to the congregation to be proactive about getting the best value for our property. The American computer company that is moving into Sandyford will need accommodation for its staff. If we lose this opportunity we could be accused in time to come of bad housekeeping and, anyway, by then the ground will be a jungle.'

'Why don't we break for a brainstorming session,' Hannah suggested. She had more handouts on discernment. But before they had time to move their chairs, de Chantal stood up. 'I'm weary of discernment and brainstorming and finding God verbiage,' she said. 'It seems to me what's happening is an attempt to pull the wool over our eyes.'

'Good on you, de Chantal,' said a nun at the back. Others made encouraging sounds. 'I'm seventy-six, so I won't lose any sleep if you don't like what I have to say. Sister Emmanuel said at the beginning that we should guard against selling our souls. That's what we're about to do. I'm all in favour of wise investment, but this is going too far.'

Rita leaned over and whispered to Hannah, who put away her handouts and sat down with a scowl.

'What's all this talk of inner freedom and having space for God when we can't leave the dead to rest in peace? We're going to trundle the bones of poor Catherine Browne in a lorry, as if she didn't have enough – more than enough – disturbance during her lifetime.' De Chantal sat down. As one, the Old Girls applauded.

For a split second, Rita showed her claws: 'Who's going to look after us when we're no longer able to, de Chantal? Nursing care doesn't come cheaply.' And, like a faithful puppy, Hannah barked: 'It's quite common to reinter, and it's approved by all the church authorities.'

Up till now Deirdre had remained silent. As a council member she was expected to defend what this body had already drafted. She knew also that opposing Rita would shatter the veneer of friendship that had been theirs since noviciate days. But she could no longer endure the sham. 'De Chantal has offered us another dimension to this question of balancing good management with respect for our dead. Much has been made of fund-raising for the missions. No one would object to that, but have we forgotten? Apart from Providence, Nigeria and the Sudan, we've either closed down or handed back schools to the parishes. Perhaps it's crystal clear to everyone here where the money from the proposed sale is going, but not to me. I'd like a clarification.'

'Deirdre, you know as well, if not better, than the rest of us' – Rita's thin face grew redder – 'that we have to think of our schools and maintain our high reputation.'

'We have government grants. It's not like the old days, when our salaries went into the schools.'

The debate flared up again. Now, those who suspected that Rita and her supporters were trying to impose their will gained fresh confidence. Eventually, the Superior General intervened.

They had spent enough time on this; now they would have to vote, one way or the other. For the first twenty years, she said, the old burial ground had received the mortal remains of their revered dead; winter flooding from the river had caused them to move to higher ground. 'If profit is the sole motivation,' she continued, 'the Precious Blood Congregation has well and truly joined the market place. So, think carefully before you vote.' The motion to sell was carried by three votes.

Flushed with victory, Rita stood at the door of the assembly room as the nuns were leaving; she had a word for everyone. 'Nothing like a healthy debate, I always say, Deirdre.'

'Open confession, good for the soul.' She smiled back.

'Thanks for your contribution. You always bring us to our senses. But then you're a Five.' She grinned. 'See you later at tea. We'll catch up.'

Deirdre began to wade through the documents and deeds of property, and letters from bishops abroad looking for nuns. Some of the papers had been catalogued and put in boxes. The writing was faded and illegible in places.

A Reverend Mother wrote to thank the founder for money to buy blankets for the harsh winters of Newfoundland. Another gave a day-to-day account of life in Birkenhead: Mother Superior and the community were looking forward to St Patrick's Day.

She glanced through the letters from parish priests. 'My confrère Bishop O'Kane informs me that the work your Sisters do is edifying,' wrote a Monsignor Hickey from Providence, Rhode Island. 'Most of our parishioners here are untutored boys and girls from Leitrim and Roscommon; their faith is very strong, but we don't have Catholic educators. I urge you, most earnestly, Mother Catherine Browne, to consider sending your Sisters to my parish.' Then she stopped. Folded neatly between the envelopes was a tattered note. The heading read:

Henry Palmer Nolan MD
Apothecary Hall
46 Baggot Street Lower
Dublin

The copperplate writing had faded, but she made out Catherine's name, and words that stalled her examination: *lithium* and *melas melanos*. She trawled a dictionary and found what she had suspected: melancholia.

A cutting from the *Freeman's Journal* showed Oak Hill during the great flood. The report described the evacuation of Mill Lane cottages when the river burst its banks. Another cutting showed a photo of the main house: at each side, where the school and chapel now stood, were clusters of trees in leaf. Surprised by the camera, two men at work in a flowerbed looked up from their digging. The paper ended its two-column piece by paying tribute to Catherine and her community:

> Mother Catherine Browne and her lady companions have become a familiar sight on dark mornings winding their way down Herbert's Lane to the village for Mass. They follow the leader, who holds a lantern. Mother Catherine Browne, a distinguished lady, is the only daughter of the Hon Richard Browne, landowner, of Sackville Park, Navan, County Meath. Her brother, Thomas, who was solicitor general, has recently been appointed a Member of Parliament.

In a hidey-hole behind a picture of the Pope was a key to the safe, with the maker's name around the brass handle – McWirters, Stoke-on-Trent. She had to pull with all her might to open the massive door. The smell of years in darkness rose from the stacks of yellowed papers. She gaped at her discovery: hardback journals and record books, rolled-up maps and, most important of all, two companion drawers where her treasure lay. She took the diaries to the desk, pushed aside the maps and, with care, laid out the cloth-covered copies on the green baize. They were in chronological order; the writing on the labels was de Chantal's.

She read an entry dated 2 November 1857:

> I trust the Lord's wisdom will bestow on Father
> and dear Henry the strength to accept my decision.
> Marriage will never be my choice.

A twinge of conscience caused her to nibble at a thumbnail. She was violating what was private, but the archaeologist's excitement had her in its grip. A few pages on, Catherine resolves a painful choice:

> Should I return to Ailsbury and seek Henry's
> forgiveness and proceed with the nuptials? That
> would please father greatly. But alas, no, I cannot
> contemplate such a course. A thorn has been thrust
> in my side, a cross from the Lord. It would be a
> mockery of what is sacred to enter matrimony.

Over needlework, generations of novices in Belgrave had received the standard version of Catherine's broken engagement. By Deirdre's time, Henry had become the handsome suitor who had been to Stoneyhurst with her brothers and had visited Sackville Park during the summer. They had strolled through the lush fields, played croquet or debated at the dinner table current events such as O'Connell's Repeal Bill. Despite being outnumbered, Catherine had defended the merits of the bill. 'Look here,' they argued, 'we supported emancipation for Catholics, but we have nothing to gain by disengaging from the Union.'

Advancing arguments that left them at a loss for a reply, Catherine insisted on breaking with the manners of the time, and when the other ladies were making their way to the drawing room, she continued the debate while the gentlemen were taking their port.

On another occasion, she struck the table with such force a wineglass tumbled and a jagged patch, like a sketch of a foreign country, spread over the linen cloth. They had happened on the prickly topic of the day: the numbers who were being imprisoned for vagrancy.

'With the greatest respect, Catherine,' Henry reminded her, 'you seem to have forgotten that these beggars can avail of the Poor Law Act, which provides for them in the workhouses.'

'The workhouses are unfit for human habitation,' she retorted.

Deirdre was so taken with her discovery that she played the wrong hymn at Vespers. After tea she offered to help de Chantal with the flowers in the Glass Corridor. 'Why did Catherine break off with De Lacy?' she asked while she sprayed the palm fronds.

De Chantal continued to water the geraniums. 'When you read the other diaries you'll know. That's not much help, but I don't want to influence your opinion. Even before the Shelbourne, Catherine had itchy feet. She wanted to help poor children and she knew only married women could devote themselves to charitable works. And only in their leisure time.'

'So Henry was an answer to her prayer.'

'It would have been a marriage of convenience, and very likely would have run into trouble.'

'Why?'

'For one thing, he lacked spirit. She would have got tired of him.'

Her reading, when she returned to the Red House that evening, confirmed what de Chantal had been saying. In March 1858, an entry showed Catherine to be more clear-headed about her future:

> I cannot go through with this absurdity. Henry's
> forbearance with my changing moods causes me to
> be justifiably shamefaced. I know I have been
> exploiting his good nature, so I can no longer keep
> up this pretence. I have been looking on marriage
> as an escape from quarrels with father and as a way
> of following what has now become my deepest wish.

She put the diary back into the safe and began to scan the letters
and documents, as well as cuttings from the *Freeman's Journal* and
the *Telegraph*. As yet she hadn't begun to put order into her
research; she was more like a shopper unable to choose from the
rich display. It was close to midnight when she locked up and
hurried across the lawn to the back door.

After breakfast de Chantal caught up with her in the corridor.
'Strike gold yet?' de Chantal asked.

'Seems she had a royal tussle with the bishops — much more
than we were ever told,' Deirdre replied.

'When I went to Newport as a young nun, I heard the locals tell
how their grandfathers described the lady with the English accent
who wrote pamphlets against the landlords and distributed them on
fair days. And how the bishop kicked her out.' They had to adjourn
because the cleaning woman had arrived with a plastic bucket.

The following day Deirdre took down the box marked Castletown
and ripped the knot. Among receipts for cotton materials, chalk,
paraffin oil and payments made to the shoemaker were letters
from Bishop Gibbons and the official writ of dismissal from the
diocese issued on 6 January 1870.

The centenary book referred to Gibbons as a hard-working bishop, mindful of his flock, a dutiful servant of the Lord. He and Catherine were a formidable team, but 'like Paul and Barnabus, they had to part company for the good of the Church.'

During the summer months, de Chantal volunteered to help with sorting out forms and documents not already catalogued, and with transcribing letters, which were in part illegible. Nuns were coming and going to Oak Hill: those who hadn't made the break to bed-and-breakfast holidays, or to the shrines of France. The younger ones had been renting holiday homes. Those who were principals of schools, or who ran courses on home economics or self-development, had more money at their disposal, and soaked up the sun in Gran Canaria. But the nuns who still carried in their system the vestiges of convent secrecy covered their tracks by saying they were going to see a favourite aunt who was dying in London or Manchester.

At breakfast the guests recited the previous day's adventures: window-shopping in Grafton Street, coffee in Bewley's and a trip around Dublin in the sightseeing bus. They marvelled at the freedom they now enjoyed and laughed at the bad old days when they had been afraid to walk the streets after nightfall in case the archbishop spotted them through the darkened glass of his Daimler.

The reinterment took place one day at the end of June when the copper beeches were shimmering in the sun and a few girls were down on the grass tennis court, casually tapping the ball over a slack net. The nuns assembled beside the new graves, where a lorry had emptied its contents from the old cemetery. A Corporation official wiped his bald head with a handkerchief and paced up and down. Birds with cautious eyes darted for pickings in the fresh earth. The nuns sang the *Salve Regina* and *Lord of All Hopefulness,* but there was still no sign of the chaplain. They were halfway through the Rosary when the white BMW pulled up in front of the main door. The funeral bell brought the doubles match to a halt, and the girls drew close to the net as if to support each other against the thought of skulls, and graveyards, and death. They stood looking at the grim spectacle. A dog with a laughing mouth waddled into the convent grounds, sniffed at a back tyre of the priest's car and raised its leg. One of the girls put a hand to her face and nudged her friend.

Away from the sun, the nuns who couldn't attend the ceremony gathered like crows inside the lunette window on the east wing of the convent. They said the Rosary and sobbed as they looked down, where the chaplain was reciting prayers; when he raised the aspergillum to sprinkle the grave, the wide sleeve of his surplice flapped in the breeze. 'Poor Catherine,' said one. 'Why couldn't they leave her where she was? We've come to a sorry pass when all they can think about is money.' Her companion linked arms with her and they trundled off down the corridor where the sun never reached.

During a heatwave the builders invaded with dumper trucks and a lot of shouting as they set up a Portacabin. They cast off their shirts and raised clouds of dust while erecting a fence around the land and the boarding school, and outdid each other with coarse remarks, especially on Monday mornings. 'Will youse look at him? He can't get it up any more,' Anselm heard them shout at a lorry driver. She complained to the foreman. They were quiet for a day or so, apart from loud guffaws while they leafed through the *Mirror* during their mid-morning break. From then on, the nuns kept to the walled garden at the other side of the convent for their daily walk. Here the rattle of Kango hammers and drills was less severe.

One morning a caterpillar truck slouched up the driveway bearing a crane and a wrecking ball. With much clanging of metal and a cacophony of instructions, the men assembled the crane in an upright position; the ball swung from tungsten wires in a threatening way beside the dormitories.

After lunch, the young man at the controls lined up his target, but the old nuns who had been peeping out through the lunette window left before the wrecking ball crashed against the grey wall and sent bricks and mortar tumbling to the ground and a cloud of dust rising into the air. By evening, the three-storey pile was a mound of rubble.

At tea the nuns received another jolt: the chap with the Dallas cap hadn't been told about the stained-glass window to St Francis.

Anselm accosted him. 'But it wasn't my fault,' the man pleaded. 'The clerk of works never told me.'

'Only a fool or a barbarian wouldn't know that you don't destroy a beautiful window like that,' Anselm said. Turning on her heel, she barked at him: 'And if you had a screed of manners you'd remove that stupid-looking cap while you're talking to a Sister.'

After nightfall, Deirdre took a walk around the lake. Here and there, in a heap of bricks and bits of concrete, shards of her own story glinted in the moonlight. The window had become a holy place for generations of boarders. The year Anselm had taken her in hand after school and she won the Feis Cheoil for piano, she had knelt at the prie-dieu every morning, but her Novena got lost in the rainbow colours on the wooden floor. The inscription had become implanted in her memory: 'To Reverend Mother and Community from Bishop Hogan. Please pray for me.' Tall hats and women in cloaks took shape in her mind.

Rita stayed away until the grief had abated, then at breakfast one morning she nodded at their distress. 'You're right, young people have no respect, Anselm. I see them hanging around the village after school – even our own students. I have to remind them they are Oak Hill girls.' When she had been principal, she had tried to send a girl home for her uniform one morning during the Leaving Certificate exams, until Deirdre brought her to her senses, saying, 'You could have the papers on to us.'

The sisters were shuffling out of the refectory when she called Deirdre. 'I need to get out of here or I'll scream,' she said between her teeth. They might go to Dun Laoghaire on Sunday afternoon if Deirdre wasn't doing anything.

'You'd think it was Chartres Cathedral,' Rita said. As they walked down the pier past the ice-cream stand, the Stena was ploughing its way into the harbour. She hadn't slept a wink since the gloom had set in. And then Hannah was becoming a problem. 'She wants to move out of retreat work and set up as a counsellor with Zoe. For the life of me, I can't understand all this rush to be counsellors and psychotherapists. Power, that's what they want. Why can't they be satisfied with teaching or nursing? Perfectly good professions.'

'She probably wants to use her Berkeley training.' Deirdre was refusing to be drawn in. She had learned to her cost. Once, when there was no one else around, she had confided in Rita about trouble between her brother, Owen, and his wife. He had been roving again; this time Julia was going to leave him. But she'd said that many times before. Then their son, James, was carted off to hospital after getting drunk and crashing the car.

Before going out to school one morning, a few of them were deploring teenage desperation. 'By the way,' said Rita, 'how is James?' Conversation came to a halt; the others were all ears.

'Fine,' Deirdre replied, smiling to cover the shock. 'You know how young people can bounce back.'

Years of familiarity with convent ways and gestures moulded by routine made it easy for them to identify other nuns without veils or habits, walking in twos and threes along the pier: recognition was two-way. They nodded and passed on. Bríd was next on the agenda. She wanted to move to a flat on her own. 'I told her it was not on,' Rita said. 'She can go to *Spes;* there's only two there at the moment, and Cabinteely is still near her work. Anyway, she has a car all to herself, so there's little fear of her.' While the tirade continued, Deirdre began to wonder what was behind the Sunday stroll.

Then Rita issued her invitation. Four of them had planned to go to Donegal, but one had dropped out. Would Deirdre join them? The story had already done the rounds. Rita would be left with Hannah and Zoe. 'I've no intention of playing gooseberry,' she had confided in someone. 'I'd love you to go,' she was now saying. 'There's a few things I'd like to run by you.' But Deirdre had a tailor-made excuse. Her brother, Cathal, was celebrating the silver jubilee of his wedding and they were making it into a family reunion. She had already planned to take holidays during that time; she couldn't disappoint them now.

Along with his English wife and their children, Cathal ferried across from Coventry, where he had got a practice soon after qualifying at the Mater Hospital. He took a house in Castlegregory but spent nearly every day at Owen's. The family home became a railway station: CDs and videos left on at full blast, while cousins chased a ball with the Labradors around the back garden. A clash of accents disputing a foul. Owen and Cathal off playing golf. Children banging doors and opening the fridge for 7-Up.

The commonplace traffic of family life was beginning to get on Deirdre's nerves. So one day, while the two wives were deafening her with talk of Laura Ashley curtains, and Jaspar Conran and Wolfangle design, she escaped. Anyway, Julia was dumping her frustration about Owen whenever they were alone. She was going to leave him as soon as the last child was finished in college. The same story for the last ten years.

Like the hawthorn heavy with white blossoms in May, the narrow road to the village was laden with memories. Nolan's gate was where the other schoolchildren had hidden the evening she fell and Frank Buckley had carried her schoolbag. 'Is your knee all right? Is your knee all right, Deirdre?' They had been listening and rushed out, and started a sing-song:

> *Frank's goin' to marry Deirdre,*
> *They're goin' to have babies.*

At the grassy bank beside the creamery they used to compete for the best place: she stopped and saw again boys pushing each other against girls in the first clumsy response to the rising sap.

But boarding schools and teenage blushing upset the unbuttoned hours she had spent with him: searching for the first swallows or waiting to hear the cuckoo – hopefully in the right ear, for good luck.

Once, after the Holy Thursday ceremonies, he had waited for her with news about Courtney's Roadshow. They were putting on a variety concert the following Sunday night. While he talked, she caught the whiff of Brylcreem that kept his Elvis quiff in place.

'Will you come with me?' asked Elvis.

'Out of the question. You'll have time enough for that sort of thing later.' Her mother was vexed when she asked for permission. They met anyway on that Sunday afternoon, and sat in the suntrap behind the Protestant church. Bridie Gallagher was belting out

'The Boys from the County of Armagh' over the tannoy. She felt his hand on her shoulder and put up with his awkward attempt at a kiss. But *Mary, Modes and Modesty* and other books the nuns left in the chapel during retreats raised an alarm. She turned her face away and the fresh-milk taste of his breath brushed her lips. 'Maybe we'd better be getting back, Frank.' It was the right thing to say, according to the purity books.

The day before she returned to boarding school, they met at the same spot; this time she closed her eyes and forgot all about the books. Afterwards, they sat on the low wall outside Gogarty's shop. Courtneys were taking down the marquee, to the music of Buddy Holly and the Crickets. The song invaded their thoughts and his winkle-pickers began to tap out the rhythm to 'Peggy Sue' and 'Maybe Baby' on the flagstones:

'Pity you couldn't come to the concert.' He kept his gaze on the 'Players Please' sailor in the window. Children were screaming and chasing each other around naked poles. 'Can I write to you?'

'The nuns open all our letters.'

Elvis pouted.

'Sure, the summer holidays are only five weeks away. Anyway, we'll be on the same train as far as Limerick tomorrow.'

'It'll make going back a bit easier.' The pout shifted to a smile. At Limerick she would catch the Dublin train, and he would take the bus with his friends to the college outside the city. 'Before I meet the lads at the bus station we'll have chips at the Savoy?' But the sound of a car engine interrupted his plan. Sitting bolt upright at the steering wheel of the Ford Anglia, her mother appeared around the corner from the direction of the school. She seemed absorbed in her own tight-lipped world, and passed them by. But the car ground to a halt. She reversed and stretched across to open the door. 'I hope you're working hard for your Intermediate,

Frank, and not wasting your time,' she said, and then, in an icy tone to her daughter: 'Get in.'

'I am, Mrs Logan.'

'What did you say, Frank?'

'I am, Mrs Logan.'

'Oh, good.' And she jerked the gear lever into position.

'What's he dressed like one of them Teddy Boys for?' she asked, ignoring the children playing around the poles of the marquee.

'But he's not a Teddy Boy, Mam.'

Silence then until she pulled up in the gravel driveway and began to straighten the magnetic Lady of Lourdes on the dashboard. 'Don't let me catch you laughing like that again.'

'We were only talking, Mam.'

'Talking.' She sneered. 'A lot of good talking does.'

*

Deirdre now paused outside Gogarty's. The 'Players Please' sailor had been replaced by advertisements: aerobics and cookery classes in what used to be the Protestant church. Karaoke in the Dew Drop Inn every Tuesday night. On the lower right-hand corner was a warning: 'This is a community alert area.' Across the way, the chapel-of-ease was now a museum. A shortage of priests compelled the bishop to amalgamate with the main parish church. The shrill voice of her mother took on life again: 'not wasting your time.' Frank, now bald, with the waistband of his trousers supporting a massive girth. His Volvo outside Dunlea's Select Bar & Lounge every evening.

When she got back, Oak Hill was snoozing until the next batch of holidaymakers arrived. The heavy machinery had gone and only the occasional tip of a trowel broke the humid silence. Workmen were installing a lift for the growing numbers who were failing to climb the stairs. Sheets of hardboard encased the deep pit, and dust, despite Rita's pursuit of the cleaning women, covered windowsills and door handles.

Bríd returned, wearing a gold chain that set off her colour. 'Dingle,' she said, proudly displaying a sun-tanned arm for Deirdre. 'Fabulous. We went out in a boat with a bunch of Americans to see Fungi the dolphin.' She and Chris had had a most unforgettable meal one evening in a restaurant overlooking the harbour. They left the following day because Chris was anxious to meet another priest who had worked with him on the missions and was now stationed in Tralee. But they had a couple of days in the Burren before heading back to Dublin. 'I'm going to her nibs about moving to the house in Barton Road – it's practically empty now. This place is getting to me. Very soon there'll be no one left, only those in the nursing home.' Deirdre should get out as well. 'I can't stand too much sickness and death. I want to live before they cart me off.'

She was in a mood for talking. Seven years in Lagos. A steaming cauldron. Rain for ten months of the year. Praying, teaching, cleaning the classroom after school, washing and ironing heavy serge habits in the boiling sun. You wouldn't do it to a dog. And the thick black curtain that fell suddenly each evening at six thirty. Chris was the best thing that ever happened to her. 'He has kept me sane all these years. Maybe the Lord brought us together.' She had prepared the altar when he was well enough to say Mass while he was recovering from malaria in Mary Immaculate. They had talked about marriage too. 'But whatever about me, he'd never get a job,' she said. 'And I couldn't see him driving a taxi, given his background.

'Do you know what I look forward to the most?'
'What?'
'Waking up beside him. Hearing those first few drowsy words.

Or waking in the night and he's there, and I reach out and touch his hand. That can't be so sinful, can it? I mean, we don't do much.' She grinned. 'Anyway, I can live without that. But feeling his arm around me in the morning, being kissed – being told you're great – there's nothing like it.'

Her disclosure surprised Deirdre; it was a departure from the convent code that kept such matters under wraps: 'Whatever you say, say nothing.' The golden rule. And the other hard-earned lesson: 'Women talk.'

They poked through the ashes. Africa. Mary Immaculate Hospital. And the school beside where Bríd taught. One filled in what the other had forgotten. Bríd – Sister Bernard then – had left Oak Hill in the time-honoured ritual: the community assembled at the front door, singing 'Go Ye Afar.' Down by the lake that October morning, Eddie was burning leaves. He removed his cap and stood with his head bowed. Foley's driver waited beside one of the funeral cars – a shining black Chrysler. The four Sisters were going to spread God's word, so tears were prohibited. 'I wanted to help the poor in Africa,' said Bríd. 'Probably the mitebox in the school and the mournful eyes looking out at me that did it.'

Deirdre had been saved the 'Go Ye Afar' treatment. 'I'll have to admit I was a reluctant missionary, and San Diego hardly qualifies as a mission station,' she said. Reverend Mother called her in after school when she was at Mespil Road: an urgent vacancy had arisen at St Mark's High. She had already contacted her family; Deirdre should write immediately. 'They might like to visit you next Sunday. But no tears. Precious Blood is your family now.' A week later she was crossing the Atlantic in a Boeing. And the day after arriving in California, while in the grip of post-vaccination fever, she was standing before her class. Later, she found out the reason for her sudden appointment: her predecessor had absconded with a divorcé from La Jolla.

At her own pace, de Chantal continued to transcribe letters and papers, so that Deirdre's research quickened. The historical backdrop to the life of the founder was taking on substance. She learned how Catherine, now destined to be a spinster, was endowed with Belgrave along with the services of a maid, a cook and a gardener. For over three years she lived in this Georgian house, later to become the noviciate. Before the final batch of novices left in the 1980s, a nun took her easel to the front lawn, one September's day, and captured some of its special features – the fanlight window with sunburst ironwork over the front door, and the burnished Virginia creeper covering the orchard wall. Despite their memories of strict discipline, generations of novices had fallen in love with Catherine's dower house, set in from the road about two miles from Navan.

Here their founder had held dinner parties for women of her sort from Meath and Kildare. Their reading was wide-ranging: from Cicero, Byron and Milton to lighter works such as the popular fiction of the day. Blake had a special appeal for Catherine. Well into the night they discussed the thoughts of Engels and other social reformers such as Elizabeth Fry. They also kept a close watch on the politics of the day. Each year, in the late spring they made a trip to the Lake District, in the autumn to Paris. But all the while Catherine was restless. Talk about social reform was not enough. She had begun to write to the *Freeman's* about the condition of tenants.

Throwing aside a book one night, she challenged them to leave their wealth, and announced her own intention of setting up a society of women to work for the poor of Dublin. She was talking about schools and hospitals and workhouses. She would give them two weeks to decide if they would join her. As soon as possible, she was going to Dublin to speak to Archbishop Talbot.

During his constitutional from Eccles Street, where he lived, His Grace used to call on the Brownes at Mountjoy Square; on one of these visits, Catherine made her proposal. The archbishop's secretary had forewarned him that Miss Browne was anxious to perform works of charity for Dublin's poor.

'In deference to her brother, the parliamentarian, I will hear what she has to say, but I have no intention of allowing her near Dublin. The woman is highly impractical; her letters to the *Freeman's* grossly exaggerated the levels of poverty in the country,' he had told the secretary.

While Catherine outlined her plans, His Grace assumed the benign smile he had acquired during his years in Vatican diplomacy. 'It's providential, Catherine, that you should approach me with this request.' He stroked his ring. 'At our autumn conference in Maynooth, a member of the hierarchy, Doctor Gibbons, expressed a wish for the establishment of another religious congregation in his diocese.'

'Your Grace, my intention is to institute a lay organisation of women.'

His patronising laugh annoyed her. 'I admire your zeal, my dear,' he said, 'but that is scarcely possible. However, I'll not forestall your dealings with Doctor Gibbons.'

While they were speaking, they could see through the lace curtain her brother's carriage drawing up at the front door. He joined them for a cup of tea.

'Yes, Catherine,' said her brother, 'I should think His Grace's counsel ought to be given due consideration.' The lawyer in him invoked an adjournment. 'Give yourself some time to reflect on the Archbishop's words.'

'I'm sure,' His Grace assured her, 'that Doctor Gibbons would be glad to hear of your desire to work for the poor, but whether he would countenance a lay organisation is a moot point.'

Thomas Browne noticed his sister's colour rising. 'I trust, Catherine,' he edged in, 'you will be able to discuss the matter in a friendly spirit with Doctor Gibbons and reach a satisfactory outcome for you both.' Then he quickly changed tack and complimented the archbishop on his fine sermon at the Pro-Cathedral the previous Sunday.

Two weeks later, Bishop Gibbons received her in his library. He had been troubled lately by reports from his priests of subversive clubs intent on overthrowing the landlords. In Cratloe, a land agent had been dragged off his horse and hanged from one of the trees on his driveway. He would do everything in his power to stop this savagery. The presence of a lady whose brother was making such a big impression at Westminster might quell the rise of agrarian tensions. Also, he had heard of the Prime Minister's visits to Sackville Park for the November shoot. But, as advised by Dublin, he would not have a society of lay women in his diocese, nor would he tolerate her letter-writing for long.

On St Patrick's Day, Catherine and three of the women who shared her evenings at Belgrave made their way to Castletown to meet the bishop. First they went to Mass in the cathedral and heard Archdeacon Maleady, the chancellor of the diocese, denounce all who had hand, act or part in the murder of the land agent at Annaghdown. 'Hell is not hot enough,' he said, gripping the velvet upholstery of the pulpit with his chubby fingers, 'nor eternity long enough to punish their crime.'

By comparison, Gibbons was cordial. Over tea in the library, he advised them to consider seriously the religious life; however, Catherine prevailed and the bishop yielded, against his will, as a letter written on 19 March showed:

> Dear Miss Browne,
>
> We accept your request to be permitted to work in our diocese. This permission we grant with some reluctance. We are deeply concerned that a group of lay women who haven't taken religious vows should be, in the course of their charitable work, consorting with those who are not of their social background.
>
> We urge you to consider seeking our counsel in the matter of joining one of the established religious congregations, such as the Irish Sisters of Charity.
>
> We entrust your pious engagement to the Holy Family at Nazareth.
>
> Very faithfully yours,
> +Jacobus

At last, Catherine had a foothold. A few women from the town joined her lay society: wives of shopkeepers, the doctor's wife – women who had grown weary of crochet and gossip. A young woman called Nellie Higgins, the daughter of a grocer and vintner from Navan, completed the group. Later she was to become Sister Peter. As a monitor at a school in the town, she had often accompanied her father delivering provisions and liquor to Belgrave. While her father and a servant unloaded the contents from the cart, Nellie gazed at this elegant house; she longed to explore the inside, but all she could see was a crystal chandelier through a ground-floor window. On sunny days the panes of glass reflected white clouds scudding across the sky. Even the harsh cries of the rooks added enchantment to the place.

Sometimes Miss Browne appeared smiling at a back door, and though she always enquired about her teaching post, what stood out in Nellie's mind was the way her father fumbled with his cap while he spoke to this cultured lady.

The bishop's correspondences showed growing concern, especially about Catherine's letters to the *Freeman's* and the *Times*. She would have to submit to his directives or else return to Belgrave. Her diary showed how she eventually conceded:

> Despite every effort to resist pressure from His
> Lordship, I now see that we cannot survive unless
> we are prepared to become a religious congregation.
> For that reason, I have sent on the necessary papers
> to the Holy Father.

Along with six others, she entered the noviciate of the Congregation for Hope and Peace at Eastbourne, and took final vows on the Feast of the Assumption, 1868. Bishop Gibbons was pleased. She was now under his control and, if she resumed her fiendish attacks on the landlords, he would deal summarily with her.

He was off on the Nile with a party that included the Earl of Killaloe when she and her companions returned to Castletown. The rented house in which they had lived had been sold, but in his letter of congratulations on her profession, he made a present of:

> a fine residence, more in keeping with your sacred
> undertaking than the rented premises, your former
> address.

Her own description was different. On 16 November 1868, she wrote in her diary:

> At night the Sisters have to frighten away the rats. The sanitation has fallen into disrepair. The only light is that from candles, the only heat an open fire. Last night the wind howled and extinguished the candles several times. We gathered round the turf fire and recited Vespers. Despite our straitened circumstances we are rich in hope and determined to carry out our mission.

At tea one evening Anselm opened fire on priests who were dragging the church into the gutter. She had been reading a piece about Bishop Casey.

'Hard to blame them,' Bríd said. 'It's an inhuman way to live, and some of those old draughty houses aren't fit for a dog. Poor sods.'

'Pity about them,' Anselm snapped. 'Didn't they know what they were getting themselves into. And Casey was no spring chicken. The scandal of it.' She made sucking noises with her tongue. 'The old people especially I'm sorry for.'

Bríd refused to budge. 'If they're scandalised that easily, their faith mustn't be worth twopence.'

Anselm rotated the Lazy Suzy with such irritation the salt fell off. She muttered about bad luck and glared at Bríd: 'It's not fair to them, after being loyal to the church all their lives. What a kick in the teeth.'

Picking at her salad, Rita threw cautious glances around the table. 'One would think that the screening process they carry out now before they're let into seminaries would improve things,' she said, all the while keeping an eye on Anselm, whose blood pressure had been sky-high at the last visit to the GP.

'These young priests want jam on it,' Anselm continued. 'When are they going to grow up? If married people deserted their spouses, just like that, where would we be?'

'Leaving the priesthood and leaving marriage are poles apart.' Bríd ignored Rita's shake of her head.

'How can you hold up priests as an example to young people, when they're behaving in such a despicable way.' Anselm's neck had turned a deep pink.

'Anselm, they're not in the least bothered by priests – nor nuns, for that matter.'

'I know, and they're not taught a screed of manners, nor the Commandments, like we were taught. Only all this love – sharing love, spoiling love and wasting copybooks with stupid drawings – and not a mention of venial or mortal sin.'

Bríd gathered up her cup and saucer, but waited to gloat over Anselm's fit of temper. Children left to do what they like. No parental control. The other day a child had climbed all over her at the hairdressers. What would you expect? No father.

Later in the oratory, Deirdre's head was a mixed bag of thoughts when she knelt to pray. The image of Catherine and her companions in squalor: fastening brown paper to the windows to keep out the cold, huddling around the fire for Vespers – and yet so happy – stirred her blood. She had seen reflections of that joy in those of her congregation who had gone to South America; after a short rest, they could hardly wait to return to their shanty towns.

But what she had witnessed at supper seemed like a dream gone sour. Forecasts about the imminent death of her congregation took shape in her mind. 'We're on the last lap, Logan. You'd better believe it,' had been Ita's throwaway line, but she paid little heed.

She had her own self-contained world: correcting copies, helping weak students and purring each autumn when the results came out. Now she appealed to the silent altar for direction. The old nun who looked after the sacristy had forgotten once again to refill the tabernacle lamp with oil; without the red glow, the chapel felt cold and empty in the gathering darkness.

Through the dim corridor she made her way to the community room for a glance at the papers. Already the Old Girls were settling down for the night; as she walked along she could hear roller blinds being drawn, or water flowing from a washbasin. From one room came the faint strains of a Chopin piano sonata. As she approached the open door of the community room, she could hear Bríd's voice and the occasional sounds of assent from Hannah.

'I'm just saying, Deirdre,' said Bríd, 'I hardly knew the Beatles existed. No newspaper. And the only time we heard the radio was to listen to the Pope.'

'Our letters slit open was what I found most irritating,' Deirdre offered.

'The same in the States,' said Zoe, who was seated beside Hannah. 'Gee, that was a real pain in the ass.' On the low table in front of her was a pint of Budweiser. 'Good riddance to all that. Hallelujah, Sisters.' She raised her glass.

Deirdre traced the sharp tang of lemon mingling with spirits to Bríd's gin and tonic. 'Will you join us?' Hannah asked.

'Yes, I think I will,' Deirdre replied. 'The funniest of all,' she said, while she poured from the bottle of Gordon's, 'was old Gabrielle spending a month or six weeks in poverty and obedience and then saying: "For spiritual reading, each novice will read pages forty-seven to fifty-six – the section on chastity."' She did an imitation of her: '"Dear young ladies, you are to be as pure as angels". The poor woman had forgotten that angels don't have bodies.'

After a while, Rita joined them, but she disappeared into the kitchenette as soon as she picked up the trend of the conversation. 'Can I get you anything, girls?' she called through the open door.

'No thanks,' they chorused.

She returned with a glass of warm water while Bríd was calculating the small number of nuns who would be active in the new millennium.

The gin was causing Deirdre to be giddy. She began to tease: 'What I'd like to know is this: is the nunnery a healthy option for an adult today?'

'Healthy option?' asked Hannah.

'Natural.'

'I find it natural.'

'Did you never want to consider marriage, having children?' Deirdre asked.

'No, definitely not. I'd never get married, and if I did, the role of the father would suit me best. It's just not in my disposition to be looking after kids.'

'Never miss a man's strong arms around you?' Deirdre chuckled. Zoe's glance darted from one to the other. But Hannah fell in with her mood. 'No thank you, I can do fine without a strong man's arms.'

'Thank God, I never found celibacy a problem and, for the life of me, I don't know what all the fuss is about.' said Rita, who had grown red. 'And despite the fall in numbers, I'm optimistic about the future. The Lord will look after us. Didn't He promise He would be with his church until the end of time?' She looked around for approval.

'Yes,' Hannah said, coming to her rescue, 'I couldn't care less about numbers. It's quality that matters.'

Joan stole up on them. She had been out at a rebirthing

programme and was still wearing her navy anorak.

'Tea, Joan?' Rita fussed over her. She rushed out to put on the kettle, and returned with a cup and saucer.

'How did it go, Joan?' Bríd asked.

'Fantastic. Absolutely fantastic.' Joan's hyped-up description of whatever self-development course she was on at any time had become a convent joke.

'Yes, rebirthing is special,' said Hannah. 'We did it as a module in Berkeley.'

Encouraged by this recommendation, Joan gave a blow-by-blow account of how they lay on pillows and went through the shock of being born. Her eyes filled with tears, so Rita changed gear: 'We were talking about our future before you joined us, Joan.' She quoted statistics from different congregations: 'More than half the Loretos are past retirement age, but Hannah is right – quality counts.'

'The 1950s and '60s was an epidemic,' Deirdre said, smiling. 'We all caught the bug.'

'Now we haven't done too bad, Deirdre.' Rita corrected her through the open door of the kitchenette, where she was putting everything back in its place and wiping the draining board with a J-cloth.

'Speak for yourself, Rita.' Fresh from her rebirthing session, Joan was still carrying traces of anger at a world that did not give her a better welcome when she first saw the light of day.

'We've adapted well – better than the males,' Hannah said, sniggering. 'Some of them don't know their ass from their elbow.'

'I wonder if anyone loses much sleep over the future,' said Bríd. 'Let's be honest, as far as I can see, those of us who are active look after our careers, and if we have a social life outside the convent, that's a plus.'

'Do you think so?' Rita was cautious. 'Don't we feel some regret at what has passed?'

'I really miss the company. You remember when everyone was down for *The Late Late Show* or the Eurovision.' By now Joan had settled in to a cup of tea, a wedge of cheese and crackers, and two Wispa bars. 'There's a death going on no one wants to know. All this talk about handing on the torch to lay people is bunkum. All right, as Bríd says, for them with a career.'

Rita glanced at Joan's hangdog eyes. 'Yes,' she said. 'There was a great bonding in knowing that the one in the next room is going through the same.'

'Like in prison.' Bríd winked across at Deirdre, who said, 'To be honest there isn't much I miss about the past. I suppose – for nostalgic reasons – I miss Gregorian Chant. The Latin hymns.'

They reminisced until Rita began to make stretching gestures. 'We must do this again, girls.' She was now flicking imaginary lint off her skirt. 'We really should make time for each other, I always say.' She stood and began to gather up the crockery. Hannah and Joan helped her with the second washing-up.

When he returned from Egypt, Bishop Gibbons invited Catherine for tea. He had slides he showed with a magic lantern: group photos taken in front of the Pyramids. 'Look,' he said, pointing, and a gold cuff link glinted in the twilight. 'Myself and the Earl on camels – don't we look a show.' More plates showed them waving from the *Flora McDonald* as they embarked at Alexandria.

'A most enjoyable afternoon, my dear Catherine,' he told her before she left. 'It's not often I have the opportunity of polishing up my Italian.' He had shared with her the glories of the Church: Brunelleschi's dome of Florence Cathedral, Michelangelo's Sistine Chapel, where, as a student, he had spent hours lost in splendour unknown to him till then. Other evenings, he played Catherine's favourite pieces: Mozart's *Requiem*, Bach's 'Sheep May Safely Graze' and Gounod's 'Ave Maria' on the harpsichord. Once he called above the music: 'Only for Christendom, Catherine, Europe would be a land of philistines. As a matter of fact, the primary mission of the Church is to tame the savage heart, as the French Church is undertaking in Africa.' That evening, he imparted well-intentioned advice: 'You should think about lacemaking. Remember the poor you will always have with you.'

'I am obliged,' Catherine wrote in her diary around this time, 'to endure the society of His Lordship for the sake of nurturing good

relations, so I have little choice except to continue my peregrin-
ations to the palace.'

Her congregation was spreading. Nearly every month women from
prosperous families, daughters of strong farmers or shopkeepers
applied for membership. In their late twenties, they wanted to
alleviate the distress of the 'less fortunate' by working in the
industrial schools. Some were bored, some had no desire to marry,
nor could they bear the thought of being pregnant every year until
their womanly cycle had ended. In a convent they would be among
their own social class, with the prospect of doing useful work.

His Lordship was proud to have a woman of good breeding in
his diocese. At the bishop's conference in Maynooth, no one else
could boast of having a founder whose brother was such a
distinguished man. But she was trying his patience with her attacks
on landlords: why couldn't she confine herself to being a good
nun – teaching children or nursing the sick? For the moment,
however, he was willing to indulge her occasional outburst – blather
– typical of social reformers, who are reared far from the poverty
of a tenant farm. He had every reason to be proud of his own
work for the poor: hadn't he brought the Presentation Sisters soon
after his appointment? Since then he had invited other congregations. No one could say he wasn't doing his part.

Before long, Mother Catherine Browne and her ladies were
receiving high praise for their work, especially in the industrial
schools, where the pupils were preparing for the emigrant ship.
They learned how to speak well without losing their accents;
geography comprised knowledge of the towns where they would
end up: Liverpool, Boston or wherever their brothers and sisters
had gone. Housekeeping, personal hygiene and table manners were
also part of their schooling.

Invitations to tea ebbed and flowed according to his mood; nevertheless, Bishop Gibbons gave the Precious Blood Congregation his blessing. But when the letters to the *Freeman's* and the *Telegraph* took on, in his view, a more seditious character, he reached the limits of his patience.

In a rage one morning, he called one of his secretaries to the library. The priest sat obediently in front of the oak desk while the bishop waved a copy of the newspaper in the air. 'Listen to this,' he fumed. '"Women of Ireland, the words of Thomas Davis, I address to you especially. 'Educate that you may be free.' No longer abide an inferior position. You who are wealthy refrain from the demeaning practice of bringing up daughters whose only aspiration is to find a husband."'

'There's more.' The bishop stood now with his back to the fire. '"When will righteous parliamentarians root out the squalor that the poor of this country, especially women, are suffering every day. The greed of those who have wrongfully seized our land should no longer be tolerated. For how long will rapacious landlords continue to exterminate our people?'

The priest tried to calm him: 'That rant, your lordship, will fall on deaf ears. In any case, those who are susceptible to such propaganda can't read and therefore don't buy newspapers.'

It made sense. His anger abated and he looked away at the plane trees glistening now after a rainstorm. In a quieter tone, he permitted the priest to return to his work in the next room, but added, as the secretary walked away: 'I will not tolerate such insubordination from her, Father.'

'No, my lord, of course not.'

After about a month he renewed his invitation to afternoon tea, and shared his excitement about having his portrait done: it would hang alongside other bishops and cardinals at Maynooth.

That day he had had his first sitting and was still wearing the sapphire given him by Cardinal Pacinelli during his final year at the Collegio Irlandese. He did an Italian take-off: 'You'll wear it one day with dignity.'

Having dismissed his housekeeper, he poured from the silver pot and let her know he was a regular subscriber to the *Freeman's*. 'Somewhat overstated, wouldn't you agree?'

'Not from my perspective, nor that of my Sisters, your lordship.'

'But your comparing Irish women to slaves in the Roman Empire is a gross exaggeration, surely.'

'The wrongs I've witnessed can only be described in this way.'

The bishop scowled. A woman would not put him down, but he didn't want to aggravate his gout by losing his temper. 'Your reading – these social reformers – taints your critique of society. If I may say so, it conveys a very false impression. There are some very fine landlords. Yes, very fine landlords. They have done everything possible for their tenants.' From the set of her lips, he knew his words were futile. He should have taken Talbot's advice and demanded jurisdiction over her congregation.

Her letter-writing increased; she now wrote to the London *Times*, the *Boston Chronicle* or wherever she found an audience for her indignation. Money began to pour in from America and Australia. Precious Blood Sisters delivering blankets, clothes and food in their sidecar became a familiar sight around the back lanes and country roads of Clare and Limerick. An inventory in an accounts book showed the range of goods they distributed: bedgowns, flannel petticoats, calico chemises, night shifts, drawers, bonnets, bedtickers and pillows. Like hungry chickens, women and children gathered at convent doors until the nuns returned in the evening.

Bach and afternoon tea at the palace came to an end. Instead, his lordship let loose Archdeacon Maleady, who stormed up to the convent one day while Catherine was laying out a body at the workhouse. Although conditions had improved since the Great Famine, people were still dying of cholera: those who had been evicted and were too far gone when they shuffled towards the iron gates. The nuns had grown used to the smell of decay that oozed out of the damp walls and filled the whole building. Every day they fed, washed and nursed the inmates, as well as pacifying the wailing women, who were segregated from their husbands and children in the admissions block. Catherine and her companions brought the dead to be buried in the local graveyard and out of her own money she paid the coffin-maker.

Tapping the silver ferrule of his cane against the floorboards, Maleady sat stiffly in the convent parlour, refusing all offers of refreshments. Every so often, he took a small box from his waistcoat pocket and sniffed a pinch of snuff through nostrils already yellowed from his habit. When Catherine hadn't returned by nightfall, Sister Cecily, now the founder's constant companion, invited him to a share in their evening meal of bread and tea. He glared at her: 'Be assured, his lordship will be informed that Reverend Mother was out of her convent after the canonical hour.' And he swept past her and out the door.

He was back the following day to issue a further warning. 'Your course of action is in breach of obedience to his lordship, Mother Catherine Browne.' He produced a newspaper cutting and held it in front of her: 'You are the author of this piece of falsehood?'

Before she could comment, he settled his pince-nez and read in a mocking tone: 'While the condition of people in other parts of Ireland improves, the vast majority of tenants in Connaught suffer from malnutrition. Labourers refused a potato plot by farmers are dying of starvation in the workhouses. Tenants are compelled to pay rent and tithes for a few acres of miserable bog. When they fail to produce the rent for hard-hearted overlords, they are evicted and left to become wayfarers and beggars in their own country.'

He flung the cutting on the mahogany table and rapped with his knuckles. 'You'll cease immediately from writing such invectives.'

He would deal with this nun on his own. Success would gain credit with Maynooth, especially with Talbot, and increase his chance of the See when the old man passed away. Gibbons was a ditherer who should have put Browne in her place long before this. Linking the chain of his cloak, he pirouetted away from the two nuns at the front door.

'Such propaganda is not in keeping with your station in life. Take my advice: devote your time to prayer and nursing the sick. God bless you both.'

They waited until the carriage moved off and the beat of the hooves rang out on the street. Then, as soon as they were inside, they burst into laughter at the sight of the dumpy figure, only the tassel of whose biretta could be seen bobbing up and down with each jolt. '"Such propaganda is not in keeping."' Twirling around the tiled hallway, Catherine did a perfect imitation for Cecily's amusement. '"Such propaganda is not in keeping."'

From her study of the newspapers in the National Library, Deirdre noticed that the reprimand was in vain. Catherine wrote soon afterwards in the *Boston Chronicle:*

> Irish landlords failed to respond to the wretched conditions of their tenants during the Famine – that shame will go with them to their graves. They still persist in their desire to crush the poor of the land.

Scenes of distress haunted Catherine. One Saturday evening in Rathkeale when she and Cecily were on their way to the railway station, they looked on, horrified, as the RIC bundled a group of men into a horse-drawn wagon. Women in shawls and ragged children were making feeble cries for mercy, but the constabulary, their massive girths straining against the serge uniforms, marched the men like cattle up the ramp.

Standing at the door of his shop, a man in a tweed suit explained what was happening. 'These poor men came in from the country, ma'am, hoping to end their days in the workhouse. When they were turned away, they rushed the bakery.' He indicated across the street where another policeman with baton drawn was standing in front of a broken window. Catherine woke screaming that night with the dark eyes of the prisoners before her.

Through her letters she became a celebrity. She was a guest speaker in Dublin, London and Paris. Money flowed in. Hardcover ledgers showed an account of the contributions as well as the names and addresses of the donors. A parish in Springfield, Massachusetts sent her five hundred dollars.

Bishop Gibbons read of her success in the *Telegraph*. One evening in late January, while having tea with his secretary, he wiped his lips and replaced his napkin in its silver ring. 'What more can I do, Father?' he asked.

The young priest looked up from his boiled egg.

'That woman, Father, she keeps troubling my conscience.' The bishop kept his gaze on the swaying branches outside the dining-room window. 'The pastoral letter I'm now preparing for Lent shows clearly my interest in educating the poor in faith and morals. Why does she have to be so stubborn? I have no desire for acrimony – all I want is a bit of peace, Father.'

On evenings like this he longed for Rome. Opening the shutters of his memory, he recited again the same litany of praises about the Eternal City for the po-faced secretary. The Collegio Irlandese in the morning sun and the warm colours of the Via Sancti Quattro: the ochre walls and the crimson geraniums in window boxes. Walking trips on the Sabine Hills, and the purple hue from the vines on the Tivoli slopes. On the day of his ordination, in St Peter's Square, Monsignor Kirby, the college rector, took him aside and said: 'You are a credit to Connaught, Father James.' His pince-nez caught the sunlight. 'An exemplary student. Your priesthood will bring great blessings to many. Should you so desire, a career awaits you here in the service of the Holy Father.'

Poverty. Carlyle and Ruskin. He knew what poverty was all about – growing up in a smoke-filled cottage, rats nesting in the thatch and scurrying across the clay floor while his rheumatic father struggled to his knees for the family Rosary.

'Absolutely, my lord,' the secretary nodded. 'The woman is naive.'

Deirdre was so absorbed in the microfilm, she sometimes forgot to have lunch until hunger made inroads into her concentration – which was well after 3 o'clock in the afternoon. Then she went to a nearby sandwich bar and sat in the window, but took little notice of the passers-by; in her head she was following a drama of bishops and landlords and a woman battling against the odds. Her congregation had reinvented a founder. 'She was obedient to the Lord in all things,' the novice mistress told them several times during her spiritual talk every Tuesday in the chapel. 'She modelled her life on our Blessed Lady, as you are doing, and one day, by God's grace, you will follow in her footsteps.'

'I sometimes wondered what she was like,' Deirdre remarked to de Chantal one evening while they strolled around the grounds after tea. 'A cardboard cut-out: that's what we were given. I mean, what she wrote to the papers was there in black and white – a public record. And no one made any reference to it.'

'A nun who dares to challenge the authority of bishops would hardly be a role model in your day, even less in mine,' said de Chantal. 'God knows what we might have done – stand up for ourselves, maybe. Do you remember the rule about not being out after dark, and the roasting poor Joan got the night she was waiting for a bus outside the uni and the archbishop passed by in the Daimler?'

'I remember. And she had to trot off to the palace to apologise.'

Deirdre shaded her eyes and looked away towards the west: the oak trees were casting long shadows over the lawn. 'I can understand how they might cloak the diaries, but her defence of tenant farmers, poor people – that's so commendable.'

'Fear, I'd say. Fear that they might open a can of worms. And if they knew the full contents of those diaries, I'm not surprised they kept things under wraps.'

'Why didn't they destroy them?' Deirdre asked.

'Why? I don't know. The criminal always leaves a clue. Makes life a bit more interesting.'

'You begin to wonder. What do we know about anything? I mean, we're given a line and we go through life believing it's gospel.'

'Deirdre, I'm too long in the tooth for those questions.'

Deirdre stood for a moment. 'It's like discovering something about one's family. You know, a skeleton in the closet. I find I can't rest now until I get some answers.'

De Chantal's lack of enthusiasm about life's hidden ways caused Deirdre to change tack. She returned to a topic they had been discussing that morning while they were scrutinising the brittle documents. 'Catherine's experience at Rathkeale seems to have had a huge effect. That men's confraternity she started in Castletown – I've a feeling it was much more.'

'Come into the house and let me show you something.' De Chantal led the way to one of the side parlours. 'You've been seeing this piece of furniture for many years now.' She indicated a round table of dark wood beside a window; at its centre were crocheted swans with red beaks. 'Around that table she held her confraternity – except that it was something else altogether.' In a reverential way, Deirdre touched the polished surface.

Apart from Cecily, no one in the Castletown convent knew about the weekly meetings of the Land Reform. Ever since Sister Peter had praised another Maleady sermon denouncing agrarian movements, Catherine had kept her own counsel. That evening, what had begun as a fireside chat about Gladstone and Archbishop Talbot's Lenten pastoral developed into a stormy exchange, until one of Sister Peter's supporters accused another nun of being disloyal to the Church. Catherine stepped in and decided they should retire for the night. The sour taste lingered for weeks.

His Lordship became suspicious of the confraternity, but he refused to pay any attention to Maleady's insinuations. At times, despite his association with Killaloe and his land agents, he found himself in sympathy with the tenants. He would not, however, allow nuns to be involved in secret societies. She had stretched his patience by writing to newspapers, but this was the final blow. What saddened him more was the rumour that the young priest, Maurice O'Neill, whom he had sent to Paris for studies, was attending the meetings. If Talbot in Dublin heard of this, the priest's chance of gaining favour with Rome would come to nothing.

Under pressure from Maleady, His Lordship called the priest to his house – a routine visit, he told him – to discuss the number of communicants and the living conditions for himself and his curate. They talked about emigration and evictions and children without shoes.

'All matters in my diocese are of concern to me, Father O'Neill,' the bishop said over a cup of tea in the library, 'and I trust that none of my priests would withhold any information with respect to the welfare of my flock.'

'No, my lord.'

At the door, Gibbons gazed at the bowed head of the priest as he kissed his episcopal ring. He would never wear the mitre. Pity. Too caught up in secular affairs. Maleady would keep insinuating himself with Talbot and the other bishops. At the last meeting in Maynooth they were more interested in hearing what that little upstart had to say about the diocese than his views.

'We live in troubled times, Father,' were his parting words, 'but we priests or bishops cannot become engaged in any activity that might cause further distress to our people.'

'Unquestionably so, my lord.' The priest avoided his gaze.

'I'll be going to Rome in September to make my *ad limina* visit to the Holy Father. You might consider accompanying me. I need assistance now in these long journeys, and my secretary is overworked as it is.'

'That would be an honour.' He tried to read the bishop's face, but the deep-set eyes beneath the bushy eyebrows were fixed on a point somewhere in the distance.

'I'll write to you next week about dates and arrangements.' Gibbons held open the heavy door and watched the priest walk down the gravel driveway. He would not give up, even if Maleady was colluding with Talbot, who knew the right people at the Vatican. While in Rome, he would make sure that O'Neill got an introduction to his old mentor, Pacinelli, the secretary of state.

Unlike other years, when she had been teaching, Deirdre was able to take up the parish choir's invitation to Lourdes in September. She had been there twice before: brought along by her mother for a good result the year she did her Leaving Cert, and then with Ita, when they visited the shrines of France. Maeve, her friend from the choir, urged her to go: 'You mightn't get the chance again,' she said.

During the quiet time one day, the two of them walked out to Bartres, the village where the child-saint had minded sheep. Here they got a respite from the fleet of stalls with their plastic cans and bottles in Marian blue, rosary beads and gaudy images of Jesus in three dimensions: his eyes opening and closing for souvenir-seekers. They chatted in the easy way of two women whose friendship had grown over the years. At a turning on this uphill road, they rested their gaze on the picture postcard below them: terracotta roofs, an old castle and, skirting the river, stacks of high-rise hotels.

Lately Maeve had come to know a peace in Deirdre's company that was missing with her husband, and she was reaching the conviction that only another woman can understand: men trample on feelings. After giving birth to three children, now grown up, she felt redundant, except for the occasional Saturday night. Not like the golden days in St Mary's Tennis Club when she and her now-husband had started going out together. School uniform to wedding dress. The two families off to Kerry every summer, and the quip that became a byword: 'Brian and Maeve will go to the altar some day.' And each year the grown-ups laughed as if they were hearing it for the first time. A Greek chorus on Ballybunion Strand. And her mother was so happy when they got engaged; she could hardly wait to tell her friends on their way into the Church of the Three Patrons for the ten o'clock Mass. Doctors made great husbands, she said: 'So gentle and understanding'.

Sometimes Maeve caught herself thinking that love between two women wouldn't be so bad at all. Just hugging and being gentle with each other. And another woman would know how to please. Once, she woke with a start: she and Deirdre were kissing and embracing, but the sound of her husband's breathing restored her defences against the strange world of the night. Only a dream, she assured herself, as she adjusted the pillow to a comfortable position and turned to the wall.

At Lourdes, Deirdre encountered the first of her hot flushes. She felt weepy and wanted to talk. 'I never thought about things like having children – well, not much – and only when I was in my late twenties.' She took a handkerchief from her shoulder bag. 'And then what Ita said: "A waste of a life".'

'Not like you to dwell on such thoughts.' said Maeve.

Below them the city was resting before the next attack of marching candles and Ave Marias. 'Did you ever feel you've been so taken up in something that you're half-blind to the passage of time, or what's happening around you?' Deirdre asked.

Maeve knew. The wound had healed, but scar tissue remained. Perfume not hers from his jacket. Occasional references to the great work of his receptionist now as clear as a nightmare. Twenty-nine years of marriage and a grown-up family. Her world in a tailspin. Now she accepted the scraps of love that came her way.

'That too I wonder about.' Deirdre was pointing towards the basilica in the haze. 'I read a piece by that psychiatrist – the one who's always on TV. "Hallucinatory experience" is what he called it. A touch of madness, in other words.'

'Madness, hallucinations, whatever. It does something for me – the peace, I suppose.'

That night, after devotions at Rosary Square, Deirdre strolled around the basilica to the grotto; she stopped to watch women filling up cans with holy water from the rock. A row broke out. The babble of languages and their failure to understand increased the women's anger. They were on the point of coming to blows when an official intervened.

She walked on. An amber glow from the massive candles lit up the faces of those who passed in procession behind the altar. They reached out to the wall of the grotto, polished by the touch of fretting pilgrims groping their way out of confusion.

On her way back to the hotel she heard her name being called, and turned to see Richard O'Brien and an archbishop with a cluster of elderly women in the crowded street. Grinning widely and nodding his head, the archbishop was deep in conversation with the women. When O'Brien introduced her, he broke off his conversation and hissed words of praise about Deirdre's great gift of music – she had played at the morning Mass in the Poor Clare convent. But he was distracted again by the women, who giggled as they asked for their photos to be taken with him. For a moment, he put on a show of reluctance. 'Shy but willing, like a cat in a dairy,' O'Brien whispered to her. The archbishop's pectoral cross caught the street light when he moved into position to pose, flanked by his adorers. 'We love going around in the gear.' O'Brien kept up a commentary while the cameras flashed: 'This is the last outpost of respect for the cloth.'

The archbishop blessed rosary beads and cooed to the women about holidays he had spent as a child with his mother in Clifden. 'We haven't met in ages. Let's see . . . ' O'Brien took a diary from the pocket of his soutane. 'I have to accompany himself to the ceremonies, but if you have a few minutes we could meet for coffee. How about tomorrow morning?'

They had their coffee at a table in front of the Hotel Méditerranée, where they shared the small change of their days since they had met at Ita's funeral. 'Look,' he said, indicating the stream of people hurrying over the bridge towards the grotto, 'Catholic Europe on the hoof for a miracle.'

An elderly couple stopped. *'Excusez moi, monseur l'abbé. Où se trouve la grotte?'*

He stood and gave directions in fluent French. His face had become florid, but it still retained the well-chiselled features of his youth. After Deirdre had returned from America and was giving in to Aidan Doyle, she had gone to him for spiritual direction. In those days half the nuns in Dublin were attending his lectures on the Vatican Council. 'A roll in the hay is what many of them are looking for, and they don't know it,' he quipped to his colleagues in the seminary. Three of them who had studied at *Propaganda Fidei* in Rome used to meet for drinks in each other's sitting rooms of a Saturday night.

Deirdre had visited him with Ita when he was a professor at All Saints. He used to take them out for a meal, and when they returned to the seminary he regaled them with anecdotes about the pecking order in the college: how theologians looked down on those who were just teaching students how to preach. As he kept sipping his brandy, the funny side of his colleagues' snobbery became more ridiculous. 'One genius,' he told them, 'who keeps reminding us he got a first in Canon Law in Rome, complained to the president that a Christian Brother here who is professor of physics shouldn't be allowed in the dining room because he's not a priest.'

A warm breeze was now sweeping over the river and flitting through the trees that lined the parapet. 'What do you make of it all?' she asked, when the couple had left.

'At this stage of my life, Deirdre, I just row with the tide.' He had been visiting Lourdes for thirty-five years. 'Four of us came straight from Rome after doing the doctorate. Trailing clouds of glory. The ball at our feet. Usher in Pope John's *aggiornamento* or go for the mitre. Two played a safe game: they're bishops now. The third couldn't hack it any longer. He's married and teaching psychology at an American university. And when *Humanae Vitae* came out, to our shame, we went underground, and thousands of Irish women reeled out of confession boxes every Saturday night. And Deirdre…' Head raised, he was now in a lecturing mode. 'It was in telling married couples how to behave in their bedrooms that the Church lost credibility – long before the clerical scandals.' He lit a cigar. 'We were a nation of teachers' children who wanted to get on. And in those days, a vocation gave you a place at the top table. What we didn't know about Yves Congar, Rahner and Schillebeecx, and *la nouvelle théologie,* wasn't worth knowing.' He chuckled. 'Napoleon was right: "Every private carries a major's baton in his knapsack".'

The archbishop had invited him to Lourdes. 'Behind all the smiling, he's out of sorts. Another court case last week. You might have seen the photo. A parish priest – forty-three charges. And the banner headline: "Savage Beast".'

'Sad,' Deirdre commented.

'Take a look across,' he said, with a slight movement of his eyes towards the river, where a bishop was passing by, surrounded by a cluster of priests, like children vying to be teacher's pet. 'They used to say when McDaid was archbishop that the plum jobs were given out in Rosary Square.'

The bishop spotted O'Brien and came across, wearing a broad smile and carrying a briefcase. His small, shrewd eyes retreated when he laughed.

The young priests were breathless. One of them, carrying his surplice and a breviary under his arm, shared his rapture. 'Cardinal Ratzinger is doing benediction in the afternoon.' He had travelled with him on the same flight from Rome.

'Aren't we blessed with the weather.' The bishop looked towards the blue heavens and then at his gold watch. He had to go, he said. 'But I will remember you both during holy Mass.'

'Did you hear Lynch, the chap who got carried away about Ratzinger?' O'Brien groaned when they had gone. He recalled the day he had arrived in Wicklow and found his predecessor staring into an empty grate. 'I suppose I'll be all right in that nursing home. I'll meet some of my own age group.' His voice sounded hollow in the bare sitting room.

'You'll be fine, Joe. The nuns are very kind. You'll be grand.'

'I'm being evicted,' he told the cold fireplace.

The removals van had pulled up in the driveway; they could hear Lynch, the curate, giving directions. 'He did me, you know.' The old priest lifted his head and indicated the cobbled yard. 'He's ordained a wet week and he can go to the archbishop and tell him I should be retired. Then the Tall Lad arrives for confirmations and I've to hand in my gun.'

'That's the way they are, Joe.'

'I've worked hard.' He heaved a sigh. 'Tried, anyway. Winter stays a long time in Wicklow.' With rheumy eyes he gazed through one of the picture windows. 'You'll manage. You have your books.'

He gripped the armrest and lifted himself. 'Have a drop to honour the occasion.'

While the old man was filling their glasses, O'Brien stole a glance around the room. A faint smell of dampness rose from the worn carpet. The wallpaper had faded and the chandelier that hung from the high ceiling was covered in dust. A rush of feet up the granite steps broke the silence. Lynch knocked and entered without waiting for an answer. When he spotted the whiskey bottle, a twitch of contempt showed on his pale, thin face, but he shook hands with his former teacher.

'Right, Joe,' he said, turning to the parish priest. 'Action stations. We're ready to roll. Can't keep Sister Agnes waiting.'

'Give me a minute.'

'A minute.' He smiled at O'Brien and trotted off down the steps.

'You see him' – the old man tossed back the whiskey – 'he was an accountant before he became a priest. Now he's an ordained pen-pusher. He's the type that will get on in the church.'

'What became of the parish priest?' Deirdre asked.

'Joe didn't last long in Sybil Hill, but he was right about Lynch. He made it to the Vatican: some cardinal's dogsbody. Nothing between the ears, but he massaged the right egos.

'That's what we're reduced to, Deirdre: a satellite of the Great Holy Roman. And those with ability and ambition are afraid to open their mouths in case they step on a banana skin.' He stole a glance at his watch. 'Come to Wicklow some evening. You need a break from that book.' He gave her directions to the parochial house. 'I'll introduce you to my soulmate and guardian, Patmos.'

'Patmos?'

'My German shepherd.' He was chuckling.

'The name rings a bell. From the Bible?'

'Poor oul' John the Evangelist's chastisement: "I was put on the island of Patmos because I had proclaimed God's word." Don't you remember?'

When she returned from Lourdes, a bricklayer and his helper were capping the high wall that now separated the convent from the apartment blocks. That Friday evening, after locking the door of the Red House, she turned, to make her way down the driveway to the convent, when a display of leaves took her by surprise. A medley of brown, red and yellow was strewn along the lakeside path. The pale green and light blue of the sky to the west cast a magic glow on the trees that skirted the river. Each had once been a sapling from distant lands where Precious Blood Sisters had gone: American and Canadian maples, lindens from California, eucalyptuses from Australia and New Zealand, the orange-black myrtle from Providence and, sheltering in the corner from the east and north winds, the jacaranda from Africa. Any night now, the first of the autumn gales would strip bare the maples. If only time could be held in check. She cast aside the futile wish and buttoned her mackintosh. "Gather ye rosebuds" flashed across her mind; she smiled to herself and quickened her pace along the tree-vaulted driveway.

Over at the basketball courts, two girls in school tracksuits were practising their shots; the crash of the ball against the backboard or the occasional cry of the rooks disturbed the autumn stillness. Eddie was cleaning a flowerbed of dried stalks. He had come up in conversation at dinner that day. 'We'd love to keep him on, of course, but we can't afford it,' Rita announced.

'And what will he do?' Deirdre had asked.

'Hasn't he the pension?'

'After all his years with us?'

'He was given a just wage. Remember, it's not our money.'

'Ave Maria, gratia plena,' rose from the oratory as Deirdre approached the back door. Vespers had slipped her mind. A scolding voice from the past hissed in her ear, but she refused to follow and, instead, climbed the back stairs to her room. Through the half-open door of the library, she caught sight of the glass-doored bookshelves and the wooden panels, which had been polished by generations of novices. The smell of books and furniture caused the years to dissolve. She strolled into the past.

Every Tuesday, they had assembled in this room, where they knelt in choir formation and waited for the Reverend Mother to begin the Chapter of Faults. Deirdre stopped by the bookcases: Rodriguez, Thomas à Kempis, Francis de Sales. Another shelf contained colourful paperbacks: *Why Am I Afraid to Tell You Who I Am?* When the first wave of self-discovery hit Oak Hill, everyone was reading John Powell SJ and learning how 'to connect with my feelings'. *I'm OK, You're OK* became the bible for finding oneself. Out of reach were two faded copies of *The Documents of Vatican II*, edited by Walter Abbot SJ. Her reflection smiled at her from a glass panel. The debates raged again in her head: those who were at Milltown Theology School or Maynooth silencing old Sisters with the big guns: Davis, Curran and Gregory Baum.

For the Chapter of Faults, Mother Superior had presided beneath a picture of Paul VI. 'Sister Mary of the Cross, can you help Sister James?'

'I observed Sister James swinging her arms in the corridor, Mother.'

'Sister Ambrose, can you help Sister Thomas Aquinas?'

'I observed Sister Thomas Aquinas banging doors, Mother.'

'Sister Jerome, can you help Sister Mary Magdalen?'

'I observed Sister Mary Magdalen neglecting other Sisters at the table, Mother.'

And the day Hannah had stunned her: 'Sister Mary Placidus, can you help Sister Germanus.'

'I observed Sister Germanus not flushing the toilet, Mother.'

A couple of evenings before, Deirdre had gone to the toilet near the oratory to remove a pebble from her sandal during the Forty Hours' Adoration, while Hannah had been mooching in the corridor between visits to the Blessed Sacrament.

'My oh my, Sister Germanus,' whispered Ita at recreation, 'we're becoming very careless in our personal habits.'

Deirdre took out *The Introduction to the Devout Life* and leafed through time. The spiritual director reading the Divine Office in the walled garden flickered again. Keeping a finger between the pages, he approached her while she cut flowers for the May altar. 'So edifying to see a beautiful girl giving her life to God,' he said. She looked up. Raindrops fell on the black cover of his breviary. 'We must take shelter, Sister. The glasshouse.' She placed the secateurs on the pages of the *Sunday Press,* where a bunch of lilies lay. He dusted a bench and asked her to come and tell him about her life. An arm crept round her shoulder. 'No need to be afraid, Sister.' His voice was urgent; then, all of a sudden, he kissed her on the lips. 'This is perfectly natural. Never forget you are a woman before you are a nun.' But she avoided his wine breath. It was so lonely in Africa, she heard him say above the thumping of her heart. Long nights and no company except other priests who stayed in their rooms or disappeared into the darkness – probably had a woman somewhere. Life is like that. You can't deny what is human.

'Isn't that a grand perfume from the flowers after the shower of rain.' He began to inhale in an exaggerated way through his nose. 'Ah, the wonders of nature.'

'Yes, the wonders of nature.'

When his grip became more urgent she wriggled out of his

arm and stood up. 'The rain has stopped, Father. I'll have to take in the flowers.'

'You'll come to me for spiritual direction, won't you, Sister Germanus?'

'I will.'

But she refused when he asked for her.

'Too high and mighty, is that it? Only a Jesuit will do?' The novice mistress sat behind the desk, wringing her hands. Her moustache grew darker when she was angry. But Deirdre insisted on choosing her own confessor: an inviolable right of every nun. Others refused also and soon the spiritual director returned to lonely Africa and his confrères who had women somewhere in the darkness.

That Friday evening, Bríd breezed into the refectory in her weekend casuals: tracksuit and Reeboks. 'Who closed the front gate again?' she asked. 'A guy nearly crashed in to me while I was getting out to open it.'

'The gate has to be kept closed,' said Anselm, as she whipped the lid off her carton of yoghurt. 'We can't have every Tom, Dick and Harry parking in the convent.' Whenever the Tesco car park was full, shoppers sneaked into Oak Hill, and then rushed to the bank, or collected clothes from the dry-cleaners across the road. She had taken it upon herself to patrol the grounds and expel erring motorists with a scowl and a flick of her hand, as if she was shooing away a flock of birds. 'Young people especially have to be taught a lesson. They can't take private property for granted.' She slipped into her favourite topic: lack of parental control.

A few days before, she had nearly been knocked down by a first-year chasing a tennis ball. The child was in the act of running back to her friends when she screamed: 'Come back here! What do you say?'

'Sorry.'

'Sorry what?'

'Sorry, Sister.'

'Say, "Excuse me, Sister".'

'Excuse me, Sister.'

'Go on.' She lowered her voice in frustration. 'How some of you get in here at all baffles me.'

'No discipline,' she was now saying to Bríd, giving a twist to her mouth. 'It's the reason why the church is in crisis. They won't listen to the Pope, or the archbishop. I saw the poor man the other day at the Pro-Cathedral and he looks so downcast.'

The nun who always sat beside her added topspin: 'And if we hadn't brought in these highfalutin ideas about co-responsibility we'd have been a lot better off and we'd never have lost the number we did. These silly notions came from America, and look what happened there: San Diego cleared out, and then Los Angeles, all in one summer.'

Keeping at a safe distance, Rita stacked up her side plate and her cup and saucer and disappeared to the wash-up area. 'Okey-dokey, I'm off.'

'You have to have rules, Bríd. They served us well for generations,' Anselm continued.

'Including those who end up going to Confession every second day, or else having to trot off to a shrink.'

'Everyone knows,' Anselm made her case to the lazy Susan, 'when rules are relaxed, Sisters begin to live like single women – that's until they hike off with a priest or a Brother. You need rules to curb the flesh.' She appealed to Deirdre: 'You were in San Diego when we closed St Mark's. That's Vatican II for you.'

'They might have left anyway, Anselm.'

'How many of them met priests while doing one of those courses on self-development? Paula absconded with one of the parents.'

'That's not the way I remember them. They all worked hard. And if the training was that effective, why was it so easily cast aside?'

Anselm retreated: 'Oh, I'm not blaming them. It's just that the changes were too sudden.'

She had been Superior at St Mark's, a brownstone convent at

the corner of Roosevelt and Hope. One evening, the young nuns, in a flurry of excitement before the summer holidays, started picking oranges off one of the trees in the back garden and throwing them at each other. After night prayer, she began to read the riot act until Liz cut in: 'Anselm, are you off your trolley? We're not novices any more, and this isn't Oak Hill. You're talking to five qualified teachers. So get a grip.' As soon as Anselm was called home for refusing to carry out the changes of the Vatican Council, Deirdre and the others wore summer frocks and sling-backs. Priests came to swim in the pool and stayed for dinner. During the long holidays, they moved back the furniture and danced together.

One evening, a pastor at Corpus Christi came along. He helped Deirdre to prepare the salad while the rest were chattering around the barbecue. He was back a week later with a fan. 'You said the air conditioning was faulty in your classroom,' he commented.

'I must have seemed a right moan.' She blushed. He was in a hurry to join the other priests at the San Diego Country Club, but asked if she would like to come out for dinner some evening.

They held a farewell party the following June. Again the mats were rolled up for Irish sets and, later, for John Denver and Charlie Pride – the slow numbers.

Late in the night, the two of them strolled out and sat beside the pool. Crickets were making a racket somewhere in the palms and the bougainvillea. Inside the patio doors, a low-volume John Denver had packed his bags and was ready to go. Two couples were out on the floor, the others moving about with glasses in their hands or lazing on the couch. When they spoke, it seemed like a dumb show.

A half-moon rested on the surface of the swimming pool. They sat for a while, as if paying silent respects to the good times. Now and again a ribbon of smoke rose from the dying embers in the barbecue and the smell of charred meat floated in their direction. 'On my way down, I stopped at Carlsbad,' he said in a low voice, so as not to break the spell. 'The sea was so calm and someone was playing a piano in a beach-house. "Danny Boy". Can you believe it?' He drained his glass. 'Do you think you'll be out this way again?'

'Unlikely. We're closing down Los Angeles also. Unless they send me to Providence.'

'We'll meet next summer when I go back home on vacation.' The golf-and-hard-drinking mask he wore, along with other Irish priests, had slipped. No jokes now. The others were preparing to leave, but he was in no hurry. By the dim light of the pool, they chatted on in blessed seclusion. 'You don't have to go if you don't want to. There are a couple of empty rooms,' she heard herself saying.

They switched off the lights and left the crickets to sizzle in the dark, and as they made their way down the corridor, they could hear car doors shutting and final farewells being made: 'Inisbofin then, next June. I'll hold you to that.'

'Sorry about the mess,' she whispered, and removed suitcases from the bed. He wasn't listening. 'Stay, Deirdre.' His whiskey breath drew nearer. 'Let's have a last few hours together and then go to Mission Valley for breakfast before the others get up.' She looked at him and was about to scorn such an improper suggestion, but then noticed the hangdog look on his face.

'Oh God,' was her first reaction when she woke. 'What have I done?' She was staring at the moles on his tanned back, and was magnifying each gesture of the previous night. What filled her with anxiety most of all was the spontaneity of her response, as if, in a moment, she had scant regard for all the rules and regulations that had informed her training until then. And out of nowhere came the mortal sin that had haunted her for months when she was a child. On a Sunday morning in the pantry she had licked the jelly-dipped spoon and broken her fast but had still gone to Communion. Now the axe had fallen again. Grave matter, clear knowledge and full consent. Guilty on all counts. She tried to calm the whirl of activity in her brain. After all, they hadn't gone the whole way, and on a last night people do foolish things. And she had never done anything like that in her life.

He stirred and turned to put his arm around her, but she whispered that they would need to get going for Mission Valley. In her dressing gown she tiptoed to her room and tried to keep the hangover at bay while getting ready. Then she returned to wake him up, calling his name in a hushed tone, as though she didn't want to disturb her sleeping companions.

The day was a blur: checking her baggage and travel forms, and saying goodbye to Ann and Liz, who took her to the airport. That week they were moving to an apartment. Not until she was on the plane to New York did her transgression of the night before well up again. She eased back the headrest and tried to sleep it off, but in that no man's land beyond the boundary of rational thought, her mother, the novice mistress and the devil-at-dances priest stood over her, pointing a finger. The rumble of a trolley woke her. She nursed a gin and tonic and gazed down at sun-baked America. A glistening river twisted and turned through hilly terrain like puckered brown paper. Her thoughts meandered. California. Toyland. Christmas day on the beach: history now. Tomorrow, normal life would resume.

'I'm so glad to have got that rain-sodden country out of my system,' said Liz one golden evening when they were driving home from Palm Springs. 'How could you ever think of going back, Dee?' And she needed to thaw out, they had told her that night when Ann had tried out an encounter session from her psychology course at UCLA. 'Forget Oak Hill,' they had said. Ann gave each of them a diagram of concentric circles. Who is in the inner circle of your life? They sat around on cushions and shared. Deirdre's inner circle was blank. 'Come on, Dee. This is the U S of A,' said Liz. 'We all have someone special out here.' In a roundabout way they were repeating Millar's derisive nickname – Sister Prim – which she had had ever since making light of his cajolery one summer's evening down at the croquet court, when he had lingered after Benediction.

She handed back the empty glass to the stewardess and promised God she would go to Confession as soon as she returned to Ireland. And she stared down again at another glistening serpent. God is compassionate. And anyway, the night before was the nearest she would ever get to lovemaking.

For some time Archdeacon Maleady had suspected that Catherine and another nun were hosting meetings for 'an agrarian mob'. He lurked in the shadows until he found an informer. Now Gibbons would have no excuse to defer her expulsion. He summoned his manservant to get ready his outside car and horse, and they went post-haste to the bishop's palace.

'You claim, Archdeacon, that Mother Catherine is presiding at meetings of the Land Reform in her convent. I am slow to believe such an allegation.' The bishop remained seated behind his desk.

'I can produce a witness, my lord.'

'That won't be necessary. We don't want to cause dissension in the diocese. The Land Reform, as you are aware, has some support within the Church. Bishop Hogan, for one. And others among my colleagues.'

'A view not shared by Cardinal Talbot, my lord.'

'With respect to his eminence, most of his flock are not tenant farmers.' The bishop was raging but he held his temper: given half a chance, Maleady would have a verbatim for Dublin before the week was out. He could then relinquish any hope of Maurice O'Neill succeeding him. He heaved a sigh. Catherine was the price to pay for keeping this loathsome wretch out of the See.

'I request a canonical writ of dismissal then, my lord,' Maleady demanded before he left.

'It has to be, archdeacon.'

Among the papers in the archive was a tattered note from Bishop Hogan of Ferns. The letter was dated 12 January 1870:

> My dear Catherine,
>
> I am sorely grieved to learn of your expulsion. After all your brave efforts, you above all people do not deserve such a crushing blow.
>
> Gibbons is a peacock, but not the real agent of your expulsion.
>
> I am reluctant to advise you about your letters to the newspapers or other activities; however, if you are to gain favour with Dublin you will need to be circumspect; he is a wily individual. Be assured of my prayers and support, no matter what you choose.
>
> God speed and prosper you,
> J. A. Hogan of Ferns

At the seven o'clock Mass on the Feast of the Epiphany, Archdeacon Maleady announced to the Reverend Mother and Sisters that his lordship was forthwith removing permission from the congregation to work in his diocese. He read out the document to a stunned community. One nun fainted, causing others to burst into tears in the perishing church. They had two weeks to leave the diocese. He waved aside an offer of breakfast and, while he was settling his cloak, nuns appealed to Reverend Mother to go after him. 'A Browne never went cap in hand,' was her reply. Instead she confronted him as a wintry dawn was working its way into the hallway. She would speak directly to Doctor Gibbons, she said.

'No use in wasting the bishop's time. The writ is final,' he told her.

'Then I shall have recourse to the Holy Father.'

He glared at her. 'If you take that course of action – which, let me assure you, will be entirely futile – I will see that the sacraments will not be administered to you here or wherever you go. The tabernacle will be removed from every one of your convents in the diocese, and you will be placed under interdict until you leave.'

For the next two weeks, Catherine received letters from Precious Blood Sisters requesting a dispensation; they were going to join other congregations. The Castletown community made a path to Maleady's house at the top of Main Street; they returned with glowing letters of recommendation. Eventually only Catherine, her assistant Cecily, Peter and two others remained. They sold the furniture to the Presentation Sisters, boarded up the windows and prepared to leave for Belgrave. Her world had crumbled once again.

She later wrote in her diary:

> Even Joseph, who has been a faithful servant since we arrived in Castletown, refused to harness the pony and trap to take us to the train station. I know he fears for his livelihood if he disobeys that wicked little man.
>
> We are now settled in Belgrave, just the five of us. Although why Peter hasn't gone with the others, I cannot divine. She harbours some grievance that puzzles me.
>
> The train journey was pure torture – rain lashing through a window that couldn't be closed, the carriages bitterly cold, and most of all the sight of ragged children outside mud cabins was pitiful.

The dower house at Belgrave became her home once again. Her brother Tom, now the owner of the nearby Sackville Park, honoured her rights as a spinster. He provided servants, including a caretaker, who lived at one of the lodges and looked after the house, the vegetable garden and the flowerbeds. Dusting staircases, washing curtains and putting on log fires kept Catherine and her four companions busy and helped divert them from their uprooting. In a short time, this elegant house, with its single-storey Doric portico, had been restored to the condition in which they had left it a few years before.

The microfilm in the Gilbert Library showed that Catherine had ignored Bishop Hogan's advice. For the two years she lived at Belgrave, she had continued her attack on the landlords. She kept up a cheerful appearance, and only Cecily knew how close she was to a breakdown. On 31 November 1871, Catherine wrote:

> I endeavour to keep in good spirits and not to relapse into the dreaded gloom always on the horizon. The parish priest has explicitly refused us permission to have the Blessed Sacrament in the house; as well as that, he will not allow Mass to be celebrated at Belgrave. That means a two-mile journey into Navan every morning.

But she never gave up hope of working in Dublin, even when that seemed out of the question.

The archbishop was opposed to all agrarian organisations. 'The Land Reform is composed of demons out of hell,' he had preached at a confirmation ceremony in Arklow. 'As long as I am in charge of this diocese, I will oppose it with all my might and main. I urge you, my dear people, have nothing to do with this perfidious mob.'

Three weeks later, he was dead. His successor, an administrator at the Pro-Cathedral, had also been a regular visitor to the Brownes. Maleady was the first to wish him *ad multos annos* after his consecration at St Andrew's, Westland Row. Above the chatter of bishops, removing vestments of rich brocade in the sacristy, His Grace had to stoop to hear him. Maleady would write to him about a matter that was weighing on his mind. 'By all means, Archdeacon,' the archbishop replied.

Within a week, the new archbishop had received the promised correspondence, putting him in the picture about Catherine Browne, whom he described as 'a highly unstable woman, given, I am reliably informed, to night perambulations'.

In the same letter, he availed of the opportunity to advance his own ambitious plans:

> A bishop is needed, Your Grace, who will be loyal to the Holy See.
>
> His Lordship, Doctor Gibbons is getting on in years and, according to the laws of nature, his faculties don't function like those of a younger man. So I must submit, in humility, that his successor, if such has not been named, would need careful consideration.
>
> It is well known that His Lordship favours the appointment of Father Maurice O'Neill, formerly of the College des Irlandais, Paris, and now the parish priest of Castletown. Father O'Neill is a good priest but lacks pastoral experience.
>
> Your obedient servant,
> Nicholas Louis Maleady, Archdeacon

One afternoon in April of that year, the archbishop received Catherine and Cecily at 9 Eccles Street. As they got off their carriage and climbed the steps to his residence, outside cars and ponies and traps rumbled by. A drunken man sidled along the railings, singing in a droning way about the brave patriots who had been hanged in Manchester.

His Grace received the two women in a front parlour, where the lace curtain cast a filigree pattern on the table. After a maid had removed the tea tray, he made his announcement. If she ceased writing letters and agreed to be subject to his jurisdiction, he would gladly welcome Catherine to Dublin. It was the last throw of the dice. She would need time to think. They talked again at the doorstep. A nanny passed by, holding two children by the hand; she genuflected and continued on her way, making funny faces to the smaller child. Two boys in breeches were whipping a top on the footpath. From the direction of Dorset Street came the shouts of fruit-sellers.

On the way back to Belgrave, Catherine was in high spirits – so much so that Cecily made every effort to rein in her flurry of excitement: she had seen her hopes dashed before. But Catherine's pulse was racing; she would stop writing to the papers but would not agree to his jurisdiction. 'The Brownes were never slaves to anyone,' she laughed as the train drew into Navan, 'especially to a grocer's son.' She had made a decision: the two of them would leave for Rome in a week and put their case before His Holiness.

To her surprise, she received a card from the Pope at her lodging house on the Via Labicana:

> Welcome, Daughter, to the Eternal City. We
> anticipate a fruitful meeting so that your labours in
> the vineyard of Our Divine Master may be blessed.

We impart to you and your Sisters most lovingly the Apostolic Benediction as an earnest of God's favour, and a pledge of our good will.

Given at Rome, at St Peter's, the 23rd April, 1868.

The 22nd year of our Pontificate, Pious P.P.IX.

In his violet soutane and waist sash of watered silk, the Pope's *maestro di camera* led her through a maze of corridors to the papal study, a room overlooking St. Peter's Square. The monsignor tapped and opened the bronze door and, in the distance, seated behind a quattrocento desk, was the Vicar of Christ. In accordance with Vatican protocol, Catherine dropped to a full kneeling position, but the Pope came forward and raised her up; he nodded to the monsignor, who withdrew and closed the doors behind him. They spoke in Italian about her journey; the Pope listened while she told him of her plans to open schools in Dublin. A nun brought tea.

The Pope had read some of her letters and sympathised with her defence of tenants. 'From now on,' he said, 'know that you have a friend in Rome.' He would write to His Grace about their meeting, but if the archbishop remained steadfast about the jurisdiction issue, she should place her congregation under his authority. 'Consider, Mother Catherine,' he said as he accompanied her to the vestibule, 'the Precious Blood Sisters will be in Dublin educating the young and caring for the sick long after bishops and you and I have gone to our eternal home.'

News of Catherine's good standing with His Holiness launched a steady stream of applications to join the order. She secured a house in South Circular Road, but the first postulants, like their founder, went to Eastbourne for their spiritual formation.

On her desk, Deirdre set out a faded record of their dowries; each was attached to a stamped receipt. One novice had brought enough to build the chapel at Oak Hill; another had paid for the industrial school at Ringsend.

Among the records, de Chantal traced the first constitution, drawn up at Belgrave and signed by the founder. One of the articles stated:

> Endowment or education shall not determine a candidate's suitability, nor have a bearing on the status of a Precious Blood sister. Consequently, all will be on an equal footing and participate fully in the life of the community.

The archbishop celebrated Mass at South Circular Road and welcomed the Sisters to Dublin. In a letter of thanks for her hospitality, he emphasised that the 'Sisters of the Precious Blood will have to make provision for their own accommodation and maintenance of property like other congregations.' A less formal note was to follow, wherein he let her know that 'a splendid mansion, close to Dundrum village and suitable in size and location for a mother-house, is being offered for sale.' Attached to these letters, de Chantal had inserted in a paper clip a piece from the *Freeman's Journal:*

> Oak Hill, formerly the residence of the late Benjamin A. Russell, a merchant and a gentleman, was sold by auction last Monday, 11th June, at the salesrooms of Mr Sinclair at Upper Ormond Quay for £5,100.
>
> Mrs Catherine Browne of Belgrave, County

Meath, a sister of the Hon Thomas Browne, a Member of Parliament for Kildare, made the purchase.

Oak Hill, an elegant country house, has a walled garden, a lake and a grove; the whole standing on thirty-one acres of land, held in fee and not subject to any rent whatsoever.

No sooner had he died of syphilis in the Richmond hospital than Benjamin A. Russell was buried in the paupers' grave in Glasnevin Cemetery. Of the many stories that had done the rounds in Oak Hill, the one about the jealous husband who had challenged him to a duel with pistols on the front lawn was the most often revisited. When the coast was clear, they had snatched a morsel of fun to relieve a fit of noviciate blues: 'Anyone seen Ben lately?' de Chantal asked. 'I think I saw him coming out of your room last night,' Deirdre replied.

And each Christmas, when they lit a fire in the community room where Ben had once canoodled with his women on the same chaise longue that stood innocently by a front window, the ghostly horseman riding over the lake was sure to get an airing.

By the end of the year, twenty-two women had entered Belgrave for their noviciate, and a cut-stone wing beside the orchard was built for them. Requests began to arrive from bishops and parish priests for Precious Blood Sisters. Deirdre leafed through a whole box of correspondence from the English-speaking world for schools and hospitals. She learned that, despite attacks of travel-sickness that left her drained, the founder accompanied the nuns on many of their journeys.

'Cecily,' she wrote, 'my dearest friend, only for her I would never survive the tossing waves, the nausea and the dreadful

129

headaches.' Yet her dream was finally coming to pass: the industrial schools in Dublin were flourishing. Precious Blood nuns were pitching their tents in different corners of the globe. In Nova Scotia, they were trudging the muddy streets with aluminium cans of hot soup, while in Africa they were conducting classes in the open air; for protection from the sun they used discarded sails Catherine had winkled out of sea captains. Before them were wide-eyed children, their toes scrunched in the red clay.

Despite her success, the founder was still battling with her demons of the night: in her diary for 16 August 1882 she wrote:

> Nightmares continue to be a weekly feature of my
> life. How shameful, though I conceal, as best I can,
> my humiliation, when found out on the forecourt
> again last night. Now with Cecily sleeping next door,
> and aware of my condition, I may be saved further
> shame.

Deirdre removed her reading glasses and looked out across the lawn towards the portico. She saw Cecily calming the tormented sleepwalker and leading her up the steps as dawn broke over the fields of Dundrum. What was it that kept invading her sleep, causing her such distress? Episodes from her own life came back – times when she woke perspiring: after her father's first heart attack, and then the buried-alive dreams. She sounded out Ann one day while they were washing the crockery in San Diego.

'Repressed sexual desires, Dee – that's what your dreams are about.'

Deirdre laughed. 'Freud again? I'm beginning to see why you're doing that psychology course. All those allusions to sex.'

The archbishop began to make social calls to the founder; he conveyed the compliments of parish priests where the Sisters were working. On his way out one day, he raised the subject of a good Catholic education for the children of prosperous families. Fixing his gaze on an aspidistra, he said: 'After all, they are the mainstay of the church. From them will come vocations.' Removing his silver-topped cane from the hallstand, he disclosed a fear: 'They will be forced in greater numbers to send their children to England, a godless country.'

'I received my education in that godless country, Your Grace.' She laughed.

'Oh, no offence, Mother Catherine, but remember, the poor you will always have with you.'

He was proud of the vast strides that Irish Catholics were making in the commercial life of the city. 'Have you noticed the fine houses they are building for their wives and families in Rathgar?' he commented. 'A boarding school for girls would be a fitting complement to the Holy Ghost College out at Blackrock for young gentlemen', he said. When he placed a polished shoe on the step, his carriage dipped on one side. He raised the red-tasselled biretta: 'Should I venture to suggest, Mother Catherine, that when you and the good Sisters are at crochet you might recall how the Lord spoke of the camel and the eye of the needle.'

Months passed without an entry in her diary. Then, on 3 February 1883, she wrote:

> Sailing tomorrow with Cecily in *The Odessa* to accompany five Sisters on a new mission to Hart-ford, Connecticut.

While she was away, Sister Peter, who was in charge, met the archbishop for the first time and had a most satisfying chat with him. She listened to his concern for the girls from Kingstown who were going to England. 'These young girls need a school here at home, Sister Peter,' he stressed. 'A school that will deepen their faith and cultivate refinement and good manners.' Her guarded nod spoke volumes.

After he had gone, she hastened to the chapel and knelt before the red glow of the sanctuary lamp. She thanked God for such a providential meeting. His Grace is, after all, the Lord's anointed: through him comes God's will for Precious Blood Sisters. Her purling lips worked on as the sanctuary lamp cast a deeper red in the gloaming, and her fervour suppressed any attempt by the demons of jealousy to show their faces.

But some escaped the net. She had been loyal to the founder, had plodded with her through the snow the morning Maleady evicted them. She had cut logs and planted potatoes in Belgrave until her hands were covered in blisters from the spade, but she had never been asked to accompany the founder abroad. Always Cecily. In Mother Superior's eyes, she would always be the vintner's daughter who delivered provisions to the back door.

Her conscience directed her to reveal His Grace's concern to one or two others: she asked them to pray for him. Others joined in the prayer. At first they talked in whispers about this delicate issue, but later they grew bolder and wondered aloud if the founder might not have given greater consideration to the archbishop's request. Some had been to school in England and hadn't forgotten the ache a ten-year-old feels when she is crossing the Irish Sea, nor the tears shed into a foreign pillow that night.

Rumours tiptoed around the convent: at needlework, beneath the stairs, or while the Sisters were out picking chives in the herb garden. Flies became elephants: His Grace was losing his patience. What would become of them if she fell foul of another bishop?

They had no intention of traipsing off to another congregation or returning shamefaced to their families. The Castletown remnant who had seen it all before tried to stem the panic, but when some of the younger nuns began to faint in the chapel, Sister Peter sent a telegram to Mother Catherine in Nova Scotia.

Hot flushes and night sweats continued to wake Deirdre in the early hours; she tossed and turned until the alarm clock went off, and then struggled out of bed. They told her she looked tired. 'Don't let Rita push you with that old biography. She's a user,' was Bríd's advice. During the feverish hours when she waited for the light to fill the curtains, a fiery debate took place in her brain about time and death and what she was doing with her life. Ita joined the argument. 'My days are swifter than a weaver's shuttle' brainstormed in her head and gave her no rest until she got out of bed one morning and looked up the reference in Job:

> *Remember O God my life is only a breath;*
> *My happiness has already ended.*

Had it ever begun? Picture postcards of what she had missed out on took shape in her mind, like the craving of a pregnant woman: dressing up and wearing lipstick, the feel of a man's embrace, and dancing beneath spangled lights in the Arcadia Ballroom. She had passed by one summer's evening with her mother on the way from the Nine Friday devotions in the church; they had to slow down because a group of boys and girls – her friends – were play-acting on the road. Unbeknown to her mother, she managed to wind down the car window a fraction; the band was playing 'April Love'. Pat Boone. All the girls in Oak Hill were mad about him.

She had his picture hidden between the pages of *De Bello Gallico*.

In the convent, she had followed the canon: put others first; make sure those at the table don't want for anything. When had she ever pleased herself? Two years of cheap labour as a novice when she had dusted and polished and served coffee to American monsignors when they came to say Mass and weary her about tracing their roots.

If she or any other novice let a candle fall or broke the Solemn Silence, or banged a door, they would receive the standard warning: 'You'll be sent back home if you don't behave like a Precious Blood Sister.' God spoke through the novice mistress. One of her group had clung on rather than face the neighbours; finally the doctor advised her to leave. She had to hide out in her sister's flat in Leinster Road.

Aidan Doyle rang while she was at choir practice one evening; she got his message in the phone booth. Would she meet him for dinner some evening, he wanted to know, when she rang back. He took her to Fitzer's in the RDS. The works. High ceilings, chatter of refinement and clink of cut glass. A flash of cuff links and the scent of affluence as the waiter escorted them to their table.

Over coffee, he leaned towards her in a sheepish way: 'I've the use of a house over in Ballyconneely, if ever you need a few days off.'

'Sometime,' she said, folding the napkin.

'I'm thinking of early in the New Year.'

'Just on our own?'

'Don't worry, there are four bedrooms.'

'I'm very busy with the biography.'

'A couple of days midweek wouldn't set you back much.'

'I'll think about it. Maybe later in the spring. Would you mind if de Chantal came along?'

He rested against the back of the chair and grinned. 'I give up.'

They returned to news items. The death of a classmate was still on his mind. 'Of all places, Amsterdam. With a rosary beads in his pocket, when the police called.'

'How long was he missing?'

'Two weeks. It wasn't his first visit there, either.'

He leaned over and lowered his voice: 'He took a couple of grand out of the church account. But the diocese will stump up.'

She had met the dead priest with Aidan and Millar. Once, when they were recovering from Cheltenham, he had joked: 'A bad cold. There's an old virus going around, isn't there, Aidan?'

'Wicked virus.'

Together since their days at Rockwell, the three of them seldom missed a past pupils' union or a Munster Cup tie when the college team was playing at Thomond Park. Decked out in blue and white, they cheered from the stand, while all around them the roars from the students echoed their own golden days, when they had crowded into one of the buses with hopes of meeting up with Laurel Hill girls afterwards. During the cup of tea at deanery meetings, or on the golf coursre, they tried to regale indifferent colleagues with tales of Rockwell victories at Thomond and dormitory pranks that followed.

'If only he had made contact, a couple of us would have gone over.' He was now reproaching himself. 'The Dutch police had picked him up the night before when he was refused admission to another one. Drunk as a skunk.' The schoolboy grin had vanished: he looked old and tired.

They returned to Oak Hill and sat for a while in the side parlour.

'Poor old Sully.' He kept using the more familiar name from their seminary days. 'What an end. Amsterdam.' He loosened the clerical collar. 'Sully was spoiled. We were all spoiled.'

She searched for an ashtray as soon as he took out a packet of cigars.

'It was great working in Camden Town, Deirdre. We counted for something in those days, even with English Protestants. Not any more.' A look of defeat showed on his face. 'All these revelations in the papers. The ones who were genuflecting before you would now spit in your eye.' He lowered his head. 'You open a newspaper and there's another priest or a Brother leaving a courthouse handcuffed to a guard. 'Twould make you cry.' He was returning to his home one night when a few young fellows shouted: 'Are you lookin' for a child?' And one of them had scoffed at him: 'I want to be an altar boy, Father. See you in the sacristy Father.' He had always done his best: First Communion, pre-marriage courses and visitation of the sick. His eyes grew red. 'And the top-buck cats haven't helped with their purple and their rings. Big old queens.' His chuckle became a muffled cry. 'We're a church without leaders, Deirdre. Shaggin' careerists. They look for permission to Rome before they go to the lavatory.' But he livened up before he left. 'You'll think about Ballyconneely,' and his arms were around her.

'Aidan, not here. Anyone could walk in.' But his tale of woe touched some chord of sympathy and, in the intimacy of their embrace, she whispered: 'It's a small country, you know. If we ran into someone . . . '

'In Ballyconneely?' Already he was moving her towards the door. 'Give me time to think about it.'

She took a while to settle after he'd left, and then hurried up the back stairs so that no one would notice her flushed appearance.

In her room, she tidied copies on her desk and ran a chamois over the top of the bookcase: reflex actions to deflect her mind from the flurry in her blood. Her thoughts too were jostling for attention. Amsterdam. The rosary beads in Sully's pocket. Millar's well-thumbed breviary that he left behind in the sacristy one day. And Aidan in his collar; always the collar, no matter what. A fifty-three-year-old teenager. No wonder those with drive were leaving and making a life for themselves. Nuns also. 'A ridiculous drama,' said the inner voice. 'Get out before it's too late.'

Only two left now in her year. Why did she stay? They respected her. Academic success. One of the youngest principals in Oak Hill. "Deirdre has her feet on the ground." On the ground or in the clay? They knew nothing about her struggle with faith, or San Diego or Aidan Doyle. 'Allowing him to touch you immodestly is wrong, Sister,' said the old Jesuit in the Gardiner Street confessional. 'Try to avoid as much as possible those situations that increase the chances of such encounters. But don't be too hard on yourself. The Almighty created us with such desires. And remember me in your prayers.'

'Is the air a bit stuffy in that place?' Bríd asked as they took a plate of salad each from the stack of metal dish-covers left by the cook. 'You look pale.'

She was saved an explanation: Anselm had arrived and was opening fire on single mothers who had been making their case for increased social welfare on *Liveline*. 'Taxpayers providing money out of their hard earnings for fornication,' she fumed.

'If they stopped all these allowances, it would bring a halt to their gallop,' her companion beside her reflected, slicing a banana with a vengeance. 'A few clatters across the legs when they were children would have done them all the good in the world. "Spare the rod and spoil the child," my mother used always say.'

'How right she was,' said Anselm, with a twist of her mouth. 'All this Dr Spock nonsense has driven the world mad.' Their field of attack moved nearer home: the discos started by Ita and a Christian Brother from St Malachy's.

'Discos, huh!' Anselm threw her eyes to heaven. 'I went around

the back of the gym one evening last summer. There they were –
going on with that heavy petting, in broad daylight.' Her sucking
noises started again. '"Get away from there," I said. "Don't you
know that your bodies are temples of the Holy Spirit." I wouldn't
repeat what the young chap said to me. It's the home. No prayer.
Amn't I right, Deirdre?'

With mock gravity, Deirdre replied, 'They are in need of
affection.'

'Affection. The Sixth Commandment is what they need to learn.'

Deirdre glanced across at the red face. She felt like screaming,
but instead dropped her eyes while the tirade went on. She had
lived with these women for the best years of her life, had prayed
in the same chapel, taught in the same schools, listened to the
same sermons, attended the same retreats. They had exchanged
little gifts – soap or stamps on each other's feast days – and sipped
wine or sherry in the community room when church holidays or
Christmas had sprinkled the crumbs of life's joys their way. Now
she despised their squint-eyed carping.

And in spite of her best efforts, the bad times kept sprouting
up in her memory. When the changes came and they no longer
needed a chaperone, one Superior took registration numbers and
locked the main gates at the prescribed time, while Millar or some
other priest was visiting his friend in the parlour. Then, at a
meeting supposed to be about building community, she produced
a logbook and took apart a young nun who was seeing a Christian
Brother. The detailed account showed the time of his arrival, where
they walked, when they went to the parlour, and when he left.
'When I entered, Deirdre, I didn't bargain for Colditz,' the nun
said two weeks later, as she rolled up her mattress and laid out her
habit on the bedsprings.

O'Brien rang her that evening. Would she keep an old man company for a couple of hours at the weekend, he wanted to know. She booked a car for the Saturday and drove to Wicklow. After lunch they took their coffee in the sitting room, where the smell of Patmos hung in the air. On a small table were a pack of cards and half a cigar in an ashtray; bookcases lined the walls and a dark wooden desk filled the bay of a picture window that gave a wide view of Lugnaquilla. A side window in Deirdre's line of vision showed the graveyard between the presbytery and the church. 'My *memento mori*,' he had once quipped. 'If Ignatius of Loyola had lived here he wouldn't have needed a death's head on his desk.'

O'Brien leaned back on the recliner and studied her closely. 'Those doubts that you talk about; you've weathered them before.'

'Yes, I have. But in those days, work and the choir or going to plays with Ita or a visit to Maeve seemed to do the trick. I had more energy.' She looked away at the Celtic crosses casting shadows over the neglected graveyard.

O'Brien took a sip from the brandy glass. 'Man is his desire – so Aristotle told us. What are you going to do?'

'Am I going to leave? Is that what you mean?'

'There has to be more to life than listening to Anselm and waiting until your turn comes to be wheeled down to the nursing home.'

'I know.' She began to examine her nails. 'So much is going on in my head these times, I can't make sense of it.'

'What?'

'I want something for myself, Richard. Sounds childish, doesn't it? Selfish, even.' A bird had perched on a headstone. 'Am I losing my marbles? It's as if I'm going through adolescence thirty years late.'

'My only surprise is that you haven't been asking these questions before now.'

'I did, but I had dreams to keep me going. Then I woke up and found I was on fast-forward and couldn't press the stop button.'

'Time's wingèd chariot,' he said, offering her more coffee and refilling his glass.

'Well,' she said, giving an embarrassed laugh, 'what do you have to say?'

'Advice? You'll find no shortage of people, Deirdre, to tell you what to do with your life. I'll not join their ranks. You'll have to find your own way; anything less would be short-changing you.'

He raised himself and went across to a bookcase. 'Listen to this.' He took a hardcover book from the shelves and read the lines:

In order to arrive at what you do not know
You must go by a way which is the way of ignorance.

In order ot arrive at what you are not
You must go through the way in which you are not.

She knew the piece, and after a minute the penny dropped. Eliot. With echoes of John of the Cross. 'The way of ignorance.'

'It's the only way we can learn anything.' He put away the book; they sat for a moment in silence. 'Deirdre,' he said, 'I don't have answers for my own life, never mind yours.' He raised his brandy glass. 'This by day, and Patmos to guard me at night; more from my own fears than the threat of burglars.'

'You're right,' she conceded. 'I have to find my own answers.'

She had to take Joan to the doctor the following day. Rita had an excuse. 'You talk to him,' she said in the corridor after breakfast. 'Psychiatrists give me the heebie-jeebies. They're figuring you out all the time. Like a strip-search.' She giggled. 'Thanks a mill',' and she was gone in a jingle of keys.

Joan kept drying her eyes while they waited at the gates for the Enniskerry bus to move off. 'You're so good to me, and sorry for wearying you last night,' she said to Deirdre. 'You've enough on your plate with that old book.'

On the way into town Deirdre again got entangled in Joan's troubled world. 'I did it this morning. Have I committed another sin? Should I go to Confession? I mean, if I died, I'd have to go before the Particular Judgement.'

'I told you, Joan, looking at yourself in the mirror is not a sin.'

'But without my blouse and skirt?'

'No sin.'

'Oh, thank God, thank God. And you would know – you studied theology. We didn't get that chance.' Even in her misery, she still carried the smouldering remains of a grudge. After the Vatican Council, the bright sparks were encouraged to take night courses in Trinity or Milltown Park.

'Only Doctor Harrington and yourself know me. I couldn't tell anyone else. Oak Hill, Deirdre, well . . . ' She gave a weak laugh. 'They're as good as gold, and I wouldn't have anyone say a bad word about them, but they talk. God love them, like all of us they're only human.'

'You're taking things a bit too seriously, Joan. God never intended religious life to be like that.' She was offering a Band-Aid until the psychiatrist saw her.

'You're right. But I can't stand this conscience thing. It was much better when we were told what to do. And I often think we shouldn't have done away with the veils. We lost respect. Do you remember when a man would raise his hat to you, or get up and give you a seat in the bus?' Then the click of the purse, and the rosary beads spilling into her lap. 'That's one thing I admire about Rita. To be fair to her, she fought to keep the veil. We'll say a decade to protect us: *Incline into my aid, O God. O Lord make haste to help us.*'

Two motorcycle couriers whizzed by, shouting and laughing to each other. Deirdre tightened her grip on the steering wheel. Veils. Memories of tedious meetings in the hall came winging back: flashes of anger that ripped asunder the veneer of reserve and sanctity. Long speeches about 'our sacred tradition' and how the veil is 'our badge of honour'. And Richard O'Brien sitting there patiently until the advocates of modernity had won the day. A brooding silence then for days in the community room and the refectory.

Joan broke off at the seventh Hail Mary: 'Low esteem, that's what's wrong with me.'

'What's that?'

'Hannah tells me I need self-esteem.'

Deirdre gave her a sideways glance. Her chubby hands were working at the beads, and flecks from the Kleenex lay on her navy skirt. Hannah's self-development courses were probably her next port of call. By now she had tried them all: first the charismatic movement, then the Myers-Briggs and the Enneagram; after that it was the Healing Priest, followed by several De Mello workshops at Milltown, until she discovered reflexology and *The Little Book of Calm*.

'Go easy on yourself, Joan.'

'I will. And do you know what Hannah says? "You should develop the art of conversation".'

O Lord make haste to help me, Deirdre groaned to herself. As they approached Fitzwilliam Square, Joan seemed to grow smaller, like a child nearing the school gate. 'Should I tell him about the bad thoughts I had while Father John was saying Mass? Would he be shocked?'

'Tell him everything. Psychiatrists are trained to understand.'

While she was with the doctor, Deirdre leafed through out-of-date copies of *Hello*. Princess Caroline was losing her hair, Hugh Grant had been arrested in Los Angeles, Richard Branson was going to make another attempt to fly in a balloon. The door across the hall opened and the murmur became the rise and fall of reassurances from Doctor Harrington. She replaced *Hello* on the table and, instinctively, tidied up the bundle. When she joined them, the doctor, a little man with half-lenses perched on his nose, was linking arms with Joan; he brought Deirdre into the fold. Walking them to the heavy door, he sang the praises of old Mother Gabrielle, God rest her, and Oak Hill, where his wife and two daughters had received a superb education.

They got the prescription filled at Hayes, Conyngham and Robinson in Upper Baggot Street. 'Prozac. The best,' Joan announced triumphantly, clutching the tablets as she left the shop. 'I feel much better already.' She forgot about the Rosary going home.

After tea, Deirdre went across to the Red House to read over a chapter she had just finished on the computer. But Joan kept invading her thoughts. An evening at recreation came to life. Each novice attended to her sewing while the novice mistress imparted skimmed-off news from the papers and the radio. Bobby Kennedy's death was still making headlines. The Kennedys were a great Catholic family. The president had a rosary beads in his pocket the day he was assassinated, she was saying, when suddenly a needle-box, pins and scissors crashed onto the wooden floor. Spools of thread took off in all directions and came to rest at their feet. Joan dived to pick them up. A snigger was enough to burst the banks. For a whole week, Joan had to have her meals kneeling in the refectory.

The sheaf of papers on Deirdre's desk was rising but she was finding gaps in her story. She checked with de Chantal. 'Have you found anything about this Sister Peter?' she asked.

'Peter was poor Catherine's mistake – the same as Cecily, I'm afraid, was her weakness,' de Chantal replied. 'I've catalogued all the references to her. You can read for yourself.'

While Catherine was away, Sister Peter endured the tedium of the chaplain's monologue at breakfast. As well as being parish priest of Rathfarnham, he headed the diocesan commission on education. 'I deplore the increasing number of young girls who have to cross the Irish Sea,' he told her. Peter nodded.

At the beginning, too, Catherine had sat with him in the parlour while he recounted his pheasant shoots at the Connolly mansion in Celbridge. Clergy had had the freedom of the estate ever since the parish priest there had banished the devil from the house. But she had better things to do besides listening to miracles and Old Nick going up in a puff of smoke in Speaker Connolly's Gallery Room.

Peter, on the other hand, was rewarded for her patience. The chaplain wrote to the archbishop about her thorough comprehension of the educational needs facing the country and her understanding of Your Grace's position. The archbishop concurred with the chaplain's estimate: he saw her as a most discerning woman and an amiable hostess, even if she lacked Mother Catherine's refinement.

Tired and depressed, Catherine returned at the end of November 1884. For six weeks she had stayed by Cecily's bedside, feeding her chicken broth and praying she would recover her strength for the sea journey. But every day she saw her skin turning to wax. Supporting Cecily's head while she encouraged her to take something, Catherine watched death invade the beautiful face of her companion. The telegram she received from Peter, asking her to return as soon as possible, she crumpled into a ball and flung into the fire. Oak Hill and all she had worked for had disappeared behind the blanket of fog that had surrounded Newfoundland.

The day after Cecily's funeral she took a train to New York and stayed at the convent the two of them had opened only three years before. Blind to the bustle of trolleys and children playing and newspaper boys calling for customers, she moped around Manhattan and strayed into parts of the Lower East Side where, even in daylight, women dared not venture. Once a policeman accompanied her back to the convent and on the way attempted to lecture her on the dangers of walking alone in that region. She could scarcely hear a word he was saying.

'A storm is churning up the Hudson river,' she wrote in her diary during that feverish time. 'High waves are lashing against the quay. All sailing is cancelled. Returned to Francis Xavier's with my bags for the third time. Wish to lay my weary head in Oak Hill. Ticket to travel on Saturday. Fair weather predicted.'

Having to travel steerage, she was worn out from the journey: people talking, children crying, a man singing Moore's melodies one night until very late. Someone else was playing a melodeon all the time. Her troubled head was filled with memories of Cecily and other crossings when they walked the deck or played chess or made plans for the next mission. She described the voyage in her diary:

Good Shepherd Convent, Birkenhead

28 November 1884

The Great Western brought us safely across the Atlantic, thank God. However, this new packet ship provides few comforts for those who travel aft. For almost three weeks the sound of creaking timbers and crashing waves made sleep impossible.

Placed four to a cabin, with only a two-foot-wide space for each passenger, we were a like a cupboard full of prostrate bodies.

No sooner had she set foot inside the door of Oak Hill than she caught the chill of unwelcome – not at all like the homecoming she and Cecily used to receive on their return from abroad. From the beginning, the nuns had established a custom of lighting a fire in the Long Parlour and sparing no effort to prepare a meal, punch and mulled wine. Then they listened to her account of the sea journey in *The Floridian* or *The Odessa*.

As frequent passengers, the two women had received special treatment at Tapscott's Shipping Offices in Liverpool; occasionally, the captain of *The Windstay* upgraded them to first class and persuaded Catherine to share her knowledge of astronomy. On clear nights, when the sky was star-spangled, he used get one of the stewards to organise a party to go on deck and watch while she pointed out the different clusters. 'Look, the Great Bear – Pegasus. The ancient world called the constellations after animals and figures from their legends.' She would trace a wide 'W' with her finger: 'There's the supine Cassiopeia. And Polaris the Pole star, the navigator's guide.'

As they sipped the mulled wine, the nuns listened to her

description of convent life in foreign places. Her anecdotes, spiced with imitations of the native accents, became funnier as the night wore on. Then Cecily distributed letters and little gifts from the Sisters abroad.

When they met them on the corridors or in the refectory, the Sisters were courteous and shared Catherine's sadness at Cecily's death, but the spark had gone out. Their fixed smiles failed to conceal their guarded looks. Despite her grief, she tried without success to find out why they were giving her the cold shoulder. Then after about a week, early one morning a nun knocked on her door and leaked what had been going on; she then burst into a fit of hysterical crying. A rumour was circulating, she said, that His Grace was going to dissolve the congregation. Panic had set in. The Sisters had no intention of going back home to do needlework. Though still worn out, Catherine faced the chaplain in the parlour after Mass.

'In language as sour as vinegar,' she wrote, 'he told me I was an impediment to the work of the Sisters, that I was vain and uncompromising and a constant source of distress to the archbishop by my refusal to respond to the needs of the faithful. When I questioned his authority to speak in such a manner, he told me that he had been delegated by His Grace to chastise me for my fractiousness. He added that the archbishop had reached the limit of his patience.'

Not until April of the following year did she write her next entry: 'The birds are singing. I hear Joseph sharpening his scythe, but these harbingers of spring fail to dispel my dark thoughts.'

Deirdre raised her head from the diary and gazed out at the lawn Joseph had cut in the spring of that year. Her survey came to rest on the granite façade and the front door, where generations of her predecessors had stolen a last look at the city before taking the boat for the mission countries. At least that was one battle the founder had won.

Catherine's torment was again breaking out, as her diary of 15 May showed:

> My every effort to remain calm and seem in control is exposed when they hear my screams or find me out on the landing. I place all my trials before my lord, who is acquainted with abandonment. Mr Tennyson's elegy helps me to lessen my loss. I've made his lines my daily prayer:
>
> *Forgive my grief for one removed*
> *Thy creature whom I found so fair.*
>
> How fair to me, dearest Cecily. Did my selfish demands drive you to an early grave? You might have stayed in Oak Hill had I not imposed on your gentle disposition.

'Selfish demands'? 'Had I not imposed'? Her eyes darted back and forth over the faded handwriting. Is this what de Chantal meant by "Cecily was her weakness"? She combed Tennyson's long poem for a clue. Her undergraduate days at the university came tumbling back, and the English lecturer with the canary waistcoat pouring scorn on puny minds who "Squander their time looking for worms under stones. What does it matter if Shakespeare's dark love was a man or a woman? You are students of literature. Read the text. Appraise the beauty and integrity of the poetic genius." Fine for poets and university lecturers. But this was her founder. She rang O'Brien.

'We're not all 100 per cent straight edges. God forbid.' He laughed. 'Anyway, don't psychiatrists claim that we're all a bit AC/DC. And unless I'm greatly mistaken, a growing number of our younger chaps, from the way they ponce about at clerical gatherings, are more AC than DC.'

'If it were more than a friendship?'

'Come down soon. Next Sunday, if you can. I'll get Nora to do one of her duck specials.'

Over lunch, he regaled her with clerical stories from the golf course and from Maynooth, where he still gave the occasional talk. Some of these stories he was repeating, but she put up with the flow. Like many people who were retired from the lecturer's rostrum and living alone, he held court whenever the opportunity arose. 'Mealtimes are what I miss most about the seminary,' he had told her once. 'At least you were rubbing off another human being.'

Her attention was divided. Behind him on the sideboard was a photo: a wing of his satin-lined cape tossed over his shoulder by the wind. The black and white had been taken in front of a Maynooth archway on the day of his ordination. His mother's face bore a look of triumph. 'She got what she wanted,' he remarked one day, when he had noticed her interest.

At the first opportunity, Deirdre returned to Catherine and Cecily.

'It's not the kind of discovery that would go down well. You know how the church cloaks the urge, especially that kind.' In an old-fashioned way, he had his napkin tucked inside his clerical collar. Sheets of rain coursed across the graveyard and lashed against the windows.

'So one is left with a plaster saint.'

'All I'm saying is: be prepared, if you are going to include the warts.'

They gave Nora a hand with the dishes before moving to the sitting room. O'Brien went down on one knee and prodded life into the logs; a shower of sparks disappeared up the chimney. 'The only way the church dealt with sexuality in all its diversity was to lock it in the cellar. Look at the way they handled the child-abuse thing – move a chap to a different parish.' He offered her another coffee; an excuse to refill his own glass. 'Mother Church knew about these things all right,' he grinned. 'When I was in the seminary, we'd be lynched if we were caught in another student's room So, cover it up – soutanes, veils, gimps.'

She ransacked the diaries for references to Cecily. Most were cryptic, except for an entry while in Castletown:

> Reveal to me, Lord, the nature of this strange experience. Why is my soul so troubled, if this is only a deep affection for one who, like me, is devoted to your work?

Like a surgeon examining an X-ray chart, Deirdre scanned the account of the 'strange experience' – that morning in Mayo when Catherine had knelt at the back of the chapel as the boys and girls approached the bishop for Confirmation. The smell of turf smoke rose from shawls and homespun jackets. From time to time a laboured cough, the scuff of hobnailed boots against stone or the clearing of throats broke the hushed reverence for the bishop's murmur.

Lost in a reverie of thanks to God for seeing them through a difficult year, Catherine let the scene float before her eyes. A nun accompanied each child to the bishop; another played the harmonium, while the choir sang the *Veni Creator Spiritus*.

She woke with a start to find her gaze fastened on a young nun, Sister Cecily, who was directing the choir. The black veil rested on her shoulders, setting off her slender profile. The flowing movements of her hands while modulating the pitch kept Catherine riveted to her face. She made every effort to wipe the strange yet wonderful picture from her memory, and, for a few weeks, succeeded. She no longer asked Cecily to accompany her to Dublin or overseas when on a fund-raising mission. Then she appointed her to the house for the indigent in Longford, but after a few months reinstalled her in Castletown.

'No one knew anything about that, or if they did, they wouldn't let on,' de Chantal said one evening when she and Deirdre went for a walk up around Glencullen. 'All I heard was that she put up a right fight to bring her body back from Newfoundland, but that was out of the question. In those days it took so long to cross the Atlantic.'

'But you never heard it was anything more than a friendship.'

'They said she took to the drink after Cecily died.'

'No.' Deirdre shook her head. 'No, that couldn't be. Not from what the diaries show.'

They walked on in silence. De Chantal loosened the red scarf around her neck. 'Old Gabrielle used to tell a story of Catherine's upset when Cecily asked to go to Newfoundland. She refused to go to the boat; instead she climbed to the top storey and sat there all day looking out towards Kingstown. Then she disappeared to her room for a few days.'

A gang of motorcyclists pulled up outside Johnny Fox's pub. When they switched off the engines, their English accents and the smell of exhaust fumes carried in the crisp air.

'What do you make of it yourself?' De Chantal asked.

'A few months ago, I would have been shocked. Now, I'm prepared for anything.' She gave a little laugh. 'Don't they claim nowadays that there's a sexual element to all religious fervour? Novices fainting at Benediction. Do you remember?'

'More like from the hunger or with the cold.'

'One thing is certain − Catherine did her share of suffering. And it seems her last days were even worse. I've been reading minutes from their assemblies. We thought we were split after the council. That's nothing compared to this.'

Deirdre was referring to what they had called the Black Spring of 1884, when the Precious Blood Congregation was close to the edge. By now Peter had succeeded in convincing the novices that they were squandering their God-given talents by working with the poor. Some left to join those congregations that had been founded to teach young ladies from well-to-do homes. Convents were divided; nuns refused to speak to each other; the peacemakers failed in their efforts. At times the issue became entangled in support for Catherine or Peter.

To bring the conflict to an end once and for all, the founder called an assembly on Palm Sunday. Until the evening of Holy Thursday, they disputed, in the Long Parlour, the direction they should take. The minutes showed how Catherine laid down a marker at the opening session:

> Since coming to Dublin, we have flourished, despite
> those times when our motives were impugned; our
> aims given short shrift. But we have come through
> it all and remain faithful to our promise to work for
> those in greatest need.

Some who were in the industrial schools and workhouses, even though they had been educated in England, remained loyal to the founder. But as the week progressed, it became clear that Peter and her followers had a majority.

'When Mr Gladstone grants Home Rule,' said Peter, 'we will be educating the wives and mothers of the men who will govern the new state, if Oak Hill becomes a boarding school.'

By Holy Thursday they had reached an impasse. Catherine asked them to consider the issues they discussed until they met again.

Versions of the buried-alive dream returned. In one, Deirdre's coffin had a glass lid; above the grave, clusters of people were talking and laughing. They had drinking glasses in their hands; Bríd was among them, and Deirdre called out, but again they couldn't hear.

God began to fade even more. While reciting the psalms or playing the organ, she flitted from one image to another. Dry prayer, she called her distractions, as she stared at the lancet windows behind the altar. Many of the great saints had wrestled with that for years, and it had the greatest merit before God. For a couple of weeks or so, she stopped going to the Red House and just mooched about. 'I want to think about the book for a while,' she told de Chantal.

'Are you all right?' her friend asked.

'Yes, fine. Just feel I need a break.' She had to go through this alone. Her days became shapeless; sometimes she just idled around the convent. And no one noticed, except her old history teacher, who watched from a distance. In the community room she leafed through books while the others shuffled in and out to read the papers or watch *Coronation Street*. The only blip that upset the torpor was a meeting to defer the time of evening prayer. One or two of the teaching nuns were doing a computer course in Trinity and requested the change. But the opposition got the upper hand: they would miss the *6.1 News*.

Julian of Norwich, a life jacket in the past, went dead on her.

But curiously, a couplet from Frost kept stalking her around: *'Earth's the right place for love: I don't know where it's likely to go better.'*

Although it went against the grain and broke the great convent rule that forbade time-wasting, she spent hours in her room, sometimes reading, at other times just staring at the figures change on her digital clock. After lunch, she lay on the bed and browsed through Donne's sermons on death. St Augustine's meditation about imagining one's own burial became a daily spiritual exercise for her. His grief after the loss of his young friend went round and round in her head. In *The Confessions,* she followed the saint's reflections on the gradual decomposition of the body as time and the wind erode the bones until all that's left is dust.

One afternoon she paid a visit to the nursing home. As she stepped inside the door, a nurse was supporting one of the nuns along the corridor. Every movement of her body stretched the white uniform and contrasted with the spidery figure she was helping to the toilet. They hardly noticed her in the common room. Ailbe and Mary John, who had avoided each other when they were teaching in Fairview, now sat in sullen withdrawal before the sun-blinded TV screen, where Tracy Piggott was interviewing a horse trainer. Constantine kept rubbing a chamois over a spotless windowsill and complaining that someone was stealing her soap.

'Ah, Connie,' said a nurse, 'you don't need to clean the telephone. Good girl, take a rest. You've been doing great work.' She looked at Deirdre and threw her eyes to heaven. Always responsible, Constantine had been a model for young nuns: novice mistress, bursar and assistant to the Superior General, and Reverend Mother at Oak Hill, where she did a finger test for dust as she tripped along the corridor, a rustle coming from her over-sized rosary beads. Now she excused herself to Deirdre; she had to see to the kitchen supplies. A length of lopsided slip showed beneath her skirt as she trundled away.

Reparata sat in a corner, looking out of a window, her eyes fixed on the driveway. 'Deirdre, great of you to come to see us. We don't get many visitors; everyone is so busy. You've hardly changed since you were a novice. Put on a bit of weight maybe, but it suits you.' She began about her nephew, who was in to see her the week before. 'He's at head office now, you know,' she intoned in her Cork accent.

'That's great.'

'Yes, Dublin suits them. His wife is a Mount Anville girl, you know, and she's able to send the children to her alma mater. They got the boys into Gonzaga. The Jesuits have something extra.'

'They have.'

With a rattle of cutlery, a maid pushed a trolley into the room. 'Sisters, your tea,' she announced, and stood with one hand on her hip. A streak of orange ran through her plum-coloured hair, and three studs nestled in her ear lobe. While she served those on frames, the others took their tea and biscuits from the trolley.

'Look at the cut of her.' Reparata bit into a Goldgrain. 'The skirt up to her backside. No respect. And the tight blouse on the hussy.' Sins against purity had always been a recurring topic for Reparata. Once, on the bus from town, she had given a full description of a boy who had taken out his penis in the classroom. 'Lower your voice, Reperata,' Deirdre had said, leaning towards her. But she continued as loudly as ever: 'I felt like chopping it off, you know.' A man across the aisle had put down the evening paper and was chuckling with his companion.

To take away the smell of death, Deirdre went for a walk up Mill Lane. On her way past the nunnery she heard a man talking into a mobile: 'Yes, I've got the shillings in the bag.' Then silence.

'No. No, park that until I arrive.' He was quiet again. 'Yes, I'll sort it out. No probs. Talk to you tomorrow, Mark. Breakfast stroke lunch.' A car door slammed and a booming sound thundered from inside until the engine started up and the car cruised over the cobbled yard, which had once been the burial place of Catherine Browne and her companions.

Back in her room, she picked up her breviary. The ribbon marker and Ita's mortuary card were two weeks out of date:

> *Oh, you whom I have loved so much on earth*
> *Pray for me, and live in such a manner that we may be*
> *reunited forever in a Blessed Trinity.*

She switched on the desk lamp. They had selected the prayer together in St Vincent's Hospital.

'Are you sure you want to do this?' she had asked. 'Would you not give the treatment a chance?'

'Deirdre, I'm not going to get better. Now don't make it worse for me. We're doing the funeral hymns and the mortuary card this evening.'

> In loving memory of Sister Ita Gleeson,
> Precious Blood Sister, who died on
> 24 January 1998 aged 46 years

They went through her album for the photograph. 'That's the one,' Ita had said. When she pointed, the chemotherapy drip attached to her wrist brushed against the IVAC pump. White collar over her navy habit; a lock of hair on her temple. The new look then. After the Vatican Council, they kept a watchful eye to see who would be first at Matins with her hair showing. A trifle compared with the tidal wave to follow: the special friends – priests or Brothers – who took them out to dinner and the theatre. Then the strange excitement of falling in love for the first time. *The Courage To Be Intimate* and *The Joys of Sexual Celibacy* became the new bible. Berkeley became a byword for liberation. They brought home the good news: every nun in America has a special friend and a therapist.

And with love came jealousy, deception and tears. Nuns who had been friends since the day they entered became sworn enemies when one double-crossed the other. Stories went the rounds during walks in Marley Park or Dun Laoghaire. Everyone knew about the Brother from St Senan's who had been meeting Maura, a member of the Fairview Community. They rang each other every night and went to the pictures nearly every week. They had even gone for a few days each summer to the Aran Islands or west Cork. Then he met up with another nun at a shared prayer weekend. He had now found a 'deeper intellectual and spiritual harmony,' he announced to Maura. But she could still be his friend if she wished.

After tea one evening while the others were leaving, Deirdre fell into conversation with Bríd, who was off to Donegal for the weekend with Chris. 'We may as well get some satisfaction out of life while we're still kicking, Deirdre.' She played with her friendship ring. 'For all the thanks we'll get. All nuns have been tarred with the same brush after Goldenbridge.' A bad back was her only legacy from lifting desks when she had to clean out the classrooms in Nigeria: a daily chore after school was over. 'Soon enough we'll be arguing over a game of draughts in the nursing home.' The comment put Deirdre in mind of her visit. 'Frightening to see how some of them turned out.'

'That's life. We arrive incontinent and we exit likewise, so make the most of the space in between.'

'Constantine cleaning the telephone of poisonous germs.'

'Teaches you a lesson: look after number one, or it may be too late. I don't know about you, but for me it's going to be self-management, as Hannah would put it.'

'You're a Seven, of course,' she said, smiling.

She considered talking to Bríd, but held back. After a couple of Bacardi and Cokes, good-natured and impulsive Bríd was ready to blurt out the private details of her own life. And de Chantal could do without hearing her doubts. Instead, she had lunch with O'Brien. He had been up from Wicklow that day giving a lecture at All Saints seminary – now called the Centre for Pastoral Renewal since the last five students had left to study at Maynooth.

He chuckled as he poured a mixer. 'Priests and nuns were hugging trees as I drove up the avenue,' he said.

'Probably rubbing each other's feet as well,' said Deirdre. 'We're off to Damascus House during Easter to revise our mission statement. I expect we'll hug a few trees and fiddle around with charts and overhead projectors.'

While they waited for a table, he inquired about the biography.

'I'll have a draft ready by May,' she told him.

'Will they give it the go-ahead?'

'I hope so.'

'The institution always comes before everything. Remember that.' He knew the territory. He'd been passed over a few times for a vacant diocese, although he had headed the poll every time the priests voted. 'At least they didn't make me drink hemlock like poor Socrates,' he had joked when his teaching became a worry to the archbishop, who banished him to Wicklow.

But she steered the conversation round to more pressing issues. 'It's like being betrayed. I can, I suppose, accept that they couldn't very well broadcast whatever went on between herself and Cecily, but the meek version they gave us . . . ' While she spoke he studied her face. The past year had carved crow's-feet around her eyes. 'You can sail on for years,' she was now saying, 'then time comes to mean something altogether different. You're strolling down a road and suddenly a wall is thrown in front of you; must be like coming up against retirement. You begin to wonder what in God's name you've been doing with your life.' She sighed. 'I'm not sure I want to be part of it any more.'

'You had never thought seriously about leaving?'

'Apart from the usual doubts. You know about them – receiving the veil, final profession. It was straightforward. I had a vocation. And was it such a big sacrifice in those days? Life in the noviciate wasn't too far removed from the world we were supposed to be renouncing.'

He hadn't bargained for such a weighty topic over lunch. 'Greater love hath no man . . . ' He raised the gin and tonic to his lips. 'You were kidnapped, like the rest of us.'

'It's like pulling a thread – you find you're unravelling more than you intended.' Waitresses were putting two tables together for a group of men who filled the place with talk about tax concessions and golf. 'More to do with the silence between father and mother. I've been in denial, as the Spokane graduates might say.' Dad could do no wrong. She was the queen of the land on his shoulders at a football final. With the starched collars removed after Mass, men in brown suits greeted them. 'Today's crowd wouldn't hold a candle to you,' they said, 'and who's the lovely girl with the ringlets? And do you know that your dad was a great footballer?'

'I do.'

They laughed. Away below her, Owen and Cathal trotted to keep up as they climbed the dusty track to the stadium and followed in the direction of the cheers coming from those already watching the curtain-raiser. To their left was the Gothic façade of the mental asylum.

Once, at a self-discovery weekend with Ita, she had fallen in with the facilitator's directive: Write down what you would save if the house went on fire.

'I treated the whole thing as a party game. But then a strange thing happened. I went away and did the exercise, and found that my prized possession was a bracelet Dad got made out of his medals the year I did my Leaving.'

'Psychologists have written papers on less.'

'I got this notion into my head that if I became a nun, the cold war between them would come to an end and they wouldn't split up.'

'Still, there were other factors, I'm sure, in your decision. God's way of speaking – calling. Isn't this the impenetrable mystery of life?'

'That's the nub of the problem. I'm not sure there's anyone calling. At least not in the way you put it.'

'You mean the God question is also a problem.'

She nodded.

'If anyone's faith was put under the microscope, I wonder would it pass the test? And that goes for many in religious life. But you're a questioner, and secularism is infectious.' He related an incident that was fresh in his mind from the previous Sunday. His curate had rinsed a ciborium down a washbasin in the sacristy. 'That's not a sacrarium, Noel,' he had said. 'Ah,' said Noel, 'the baby Jesus won't mind getting his feet wet.' Colleagues of his, too – theologians with giant-sized egos whose only interest was the mitre.

'None of us has superior knowledge about faith, Deirdre,' was his parting comment. 'What was it Eliot said? *There are only hints and guesses; hints followed by guesses.*'

She was on the last two chapters: Catherine Browne's remaining years, when her only support was Hogan of Ferns. She had been corresponding with him about the pressure from the archbishop.

De Chantal found his letter dated 2 October 1886:

> My Dear Catherine,
>
> I have sent a scorcher to your Hierarch. Like Gibbons, he is a good-natured man, but weak and unduly impressed by the rise of middle-class Catholics. At the table in Maynooth he wears us out about their progress. His sole preoccupation is the danger of proselytism, which danger, to my mind, is somewhat exaggerated. The Irish will never yield to perfidious Albion. Like others, he is single-minded in saving souls and ignores the abject conditions of his flock.
>
> God speed and prosper you,
> T. A. Hogan

For a while Catherine's old vigour returned and she succeeded in keeping the constitution intact, especially the article that stated: 'The Precious Blood congregation is primarily devoted to the health, education and spiritual welfare of the poorest in society.'

But the fire had gone out. In the early days she used to lead the walk around by the lake after supper. Young nuns, short of breath, failed to stay the course, even when she called out: 'Come on you lot, keep up with the old fogeys.'

Sister Peter increased the pressure when she saw the founder was weakening. By now the tension between them in Oak Hill had spread to Belgrave and South Circular Road and to other convents throughout the country. Nuns began to leave. To stem the flow, Catherine called a special meeting of the congregation. In the Long Parlour she addressed them:

> In fourteen years, Sisters, we will enter the new century. May the Almighty usher in a new dawn of freedom for our country, but more especially for the many who are destitute.
>
> The bad harvest of recent years has revisited on our people the spectre of disease and death many of us will remember from '47. For some, undoubtedly, prosperity has arrived: in the suburbs we see all the signs of material comfort.

She then addressed the troublesome spot:

> Recently some of our members have expressed in a forceful manner the need to provide education for girls who come from well-off homes. I am greatly saddened by your change of heart, but will not stand in your way.

She ended her address by saying how glad she was that the industrial school in Cuffe Street and other places throughout the country would continue to train girls and boys for emigration. She described this as 'a sad but inevitable event in the life of our people'. Then came the bombshell:

> I have considered my position at length and am now convinced that it is time for me to retire and allow a younger Sister to lead you. I am proud of you all and the great generosity and fortitude you are showing to the world.

The following day, she wrote in less buoyant mood: 'No sleep. I was away too long. A painful lesson.'

Before the vote to decide the future of the congregation, the veil of politeness was torn asunder. Sister Peter and her supporters almost succeeded in silencing all opposition. Those who were nursing the sick and dying feared that they would have to abandon their work. All the while, the founder sat at the top of the room and listened to the rising tide of anger. The war of words degenerated into a slanging match, leaving them all worn out. Catherine intervened and asked them to return to their work. They would meet again at the middle of July. In the meantime, they should pray for the grace to find out God's will.

'All my work is on the brink of collapse,' she wrote on the 14th of July. 'Even Sisters in the same community don't speak to each other. There is just a brooding hostility. Only one course of action remains open to me now.'

One of the journals with a marbled cover showed the minutes of the fateful meeting. The resolution to open a boarding school was passed by a small majority. The second crucial item on the agenda was the election of a new Superior General. To her amazement, Sister Peter received only a handful of votes.

As soon as her successor was au fait with her new post, Catherine faded out. She began to divide her time between the Red House and Belgrave. She watched while a three-storey building comprising dormitories, a hall and classrooms was erected in Oak Hill.

One of her few visitors to the Red House in the final years of her life was Bishop Hogan. Even though he had to be helped in and out of the carriage, he made the journey for her feast day and during Christmas.

'They used to claim,' said de Chantal, 'that the only reason she came back was to visit the memorial she had erected to Cecily. Back in the thirties, I think it was, they inscribed the names of all the others who had died on the missions. They must have got wind of something.' Catherine had asked to be buried beside the memorial, but the nun to whom she had entrusted her dying wish forgot to notify the gravediggers. She missed the new century by four months. The *Freeman's Journal* carried an account of her death as well as a letter from Bishop Gibbons:

> It is with deep regret that I learn of the death of Mother Catherine Browne, founder of the Sisters of the Precious Blood. May she rest in peace.
>
> In the evening of my life, I admit I wronged her. The only atonement I can make now is to confess my own vanity, and my jealousy of a saintly woman. As pastor of the diocese, I should have held out against certain parties who were intent on her expulsion.
>
> Catherine Browne deserves the highest praise I

can bestow upon her. Our Saviour asks his followers to feed the hungry, clothe the naked, visit the sick and bury the dead. All of these Catherine and her community did, with a simplicity that is inspirational. For the seed potatoes to crop their land, for the bedclothes to keep them warm, for the hobnailed boots and trousers, the people of Connaught are in her debt.

Supported by two of his priests, Bishop Hogan of Ferns celebrated the Requiem Mass, at which a number of bishops who had Precious Blood Sisters working in their diocese were present. Archdeacon Maleady, who was soon to become a bishop, sent a telegram of sympathy.

By early December, Deirdre had completed a draft copy for Rita, who was now spending more time in the Superior General's office, 'Taking some of the workload from herself,' as she put it. She fanned the pages: 'I can't wait to read it, Deirdre. You've been killing yourself. Why don't you take a few days off?'

'I have to get a proof-reader first. Maybe later on.'

'This is great. This is really great. I'm delighted.' She straightened loose edges against the desk. 'We'll grab a bite to eat some day soon. Between ourselves, I'm glad an outsider didn't rummage through the archives.'

The first indication of Rita's reaction came when she began to sit at another table in the refectory; then, after breakfast one morning, Deirdre found a note beneath her door. Rita would see her at ten o'clock in her office.

When Deirdre arrived, Rita remained seated behind a spotless desk; her crisp white blouse hung slack. She looked pale. When she spoke, her tone was icy: 'I read it.' She threw a disdainful glance at the offending object, which was on a table beside a computer. 'And I may as well tell you, I'm surprised. No, shocked. I can't get over the way you did this. To us. To yourself.'

'I can produce all my sources, if you want to view them.'

She reddened. 'Yes, that diary. Where did it come from?'

'The safe.'

'You had no right.'

'You'd prefer to hide the truth.'

'Truth?' Her voice grew shrill. 'I can assure you Emmanuel is very disappointed, but she has enough on her plate and asked me to deal with it. I've shown it to a couple of trustworthy members of the Council. Do you want to know what one said? "Is she sick, to write something like that?"'

She inched the folder away from her. 'Two sections will have to go: the insinuation about Catherine's attachment to Cecily and the final chapter about the debates. Can you not see what the papers would make of that? And we'd be the laughing stock of every other congregation.'

'Nowadays people accept that sexuality is a complex thing.'

'Nowadays people pretend to accept, but in fact are damn glad they're not that way themselves, nor anyone in their family.'

'Are you trying to tell me that in a community of women such as a convent there aren't some whose preference is other women?'

'No, I don't believe that. Perhaps in some of those convents in America: those that go on the television and make a show of themselves. Getting their names up. Not here. And I'm quite certain I've never met one in our congregation.'

'And what about the saints? Were they all perfect – whatever that means? Monica was an alcoholic: we know that from Augustine's writings. Many were neurotic. And some of the popes.'

'I couldn't give a continental about the saints or the popes.' Rita's outbursts were legendary, and all the more remarkable for one who kept a lid on her feelings. 'I've more than enough to do to keep the show on the road.'

She had begun to shout, which gave Deirdre an advantage. 'Can't you see that Catherine's struggle with her sexuality is truly heroic, given the time in which she lived?' she asked.

'Catherine, whatever she was, is not going to be the patron

saint of lesbians, if I have any say in this.' Rita regained her self-possession. 'You don't seem to realise that this could do untold damage to the high standing of our schools.'

'I never said she was a lesbian.'

'Get real. That's what most readers would take out of it.'

'So when they read the Bible, will they conclude that David and Jonathan were homosexuals? And the way David put it: "How wonderful was your love for me, better even than the love of women".'

'That's you. Always a few steps ahead. You haven't changed.' She was shaking her head. 'We're only plodders, in your eyes.' Long-buried resentment at one who stole the honours at university surfaced. No matter how late she had worked beneath the bedclothes with a torch, she had always been a poor second to Deirdre. 'Everyone knows that you don't wash your dirty linen in public,' she continued. 'Now, I have other things to attend to, and if you want this to see the light of day you will follow my recommendations.' She pushed the typescript towards Deirdre and switched on the computer.

Argument was futile; Deirdre took back the folder. In her room, she stared out at the rooftops and the puffballs of cotton wool that rose from the Pigeon House chimneys. Rita didn't have the final say: she could present her work formally to the Council, but the idea sank without trace. Some – like Bríd and de Chantal – would defend her; the rest would side with Rita. The old nuns would be confused and hurt. Has Deirdre lost her reason, to do such a thing? they would ask. For the first time, the effect of what she was doing hit home to her. How could she have been so blind? Nothing had changed.

To her surprise, when garbled versions of what she had dug up began to trickle through the convent, the old nuns, whether from world-weariness or denial, let the news in one ear and out the other. They returned to *Coronation Street* and *The Late Late Show*, and solitaire on the computer.

The reaction among her contemporaries varied. Some gave her the cold shoulder. Hannah affected sympathy, but under her breath she said to Zoe: 'What's bred in the bone comes out in the marrow.' They were demolishing a bucket of popcorn while they waited for the main picture at the Savoy. Once, Hannah and Deirdre had attended an encounter weekend run by the Jesuits at Milltown Park; at a one-to-one exercise, they had shared details of each other's family history.

The majority regarded the fuss over the book as a nine-day wonder. They had more weighty matters to consider – their careers and weekend meals with friends, and keeping a weather eye open for bargains in Clery's.

While she played the organ that evening, Deirdre watched them from the back: Joan, a roly-poly heap wedged between the armrest and the seat, Rita kneeling bolt upright, and Anselm with a renewed blue rinse, her handbag beside her on the kneeler. No sign of Bríd. Probably with Chris. But she would be back, and for all her talk about moving out, she would spend her life at Oak Hill, and return each summer after doing the Burren and seeing Fungi. Deirdre had a sense of herself as being cut off from her community, which was now absorbed in prayer. Maybe Rita, in her fury, had a point: she looked down on them. Or maybe she had swum out too far and now there was no going back.

The following Sunday Deirdre went for a walk with O'Brien along the strand at Killiney. The hint of longer days ahead had brought couples out with their children wrapped in their new Christmas clothes. 'Surely you might have anticipated this reaction. You got a shock yourself when you made your discovery.' He tried to reason with her. 'No one wants to look at the skeletons in their closet.'

'I know.' She was calming down. 'It's very frustrating, after all the work I put into it.'

But she had other irons in the fire that were in greater need of her attention. Questions that refused to go away; for one, her decision to enter a convent.

'What I said about Mam and Dad splitting up; that couldn't have been the sole reason,' she mused. 'I mean, it couldn't have remained hidden all those years.'

'Who are you trying to convince, Deirdre, you or me – or both of us? Perhaps you didn't want, or weren't ready, to see it that way.' He flung a piece of driftwood for Patmos to chase.

'So all my idealism – where does that go? Making the big sacrifice for God.'

'God, or Dad?' he asked.

'You're beginning to sound like a shrink.'

'Well, he could do no wrong – that's close enough to God.'

'That notion was well and truly scotched the evening in the creamery.' She avoided his fixed look. Clusters of seaweed lay on the rocks and, beyond them, a boat was standing on a sea of liquid jade.

'What happened?' He took the piece of driftwood from Patmos's mouth and waved it back and forth while the dog bounded, in anticipation of another chase.

'It was our first stop on the way from school.' The mysterious network of pipes and stainless-steel basins scrubbed and ready for the following morning's milk supply had fascinated them. And whenever he had time to spare, her father, the manager, indulged their wonder.

'I stole away one evening while the rest were looking in

Gogarty's window, so that I would have him all to myself.' She had rehearsed the scene in her head. He would show her how the litmus paper changes colour when dipped in the milk. Presiding on his high stool, she would watch while he held phials up to the light and explained how the cream is separated from the milk.

If he had time, he would take her on a tour of the creamery and joke with Helena at the huge butter churn. Although she hoped he wouldn't sing that silly verse:

> *Won't you come out tonight, Helena,*
> *Any chance of the concertina?*

To surprise him, she crept along by the wall, being careful not to scuff her summer scandals against the gravel. As she inched closer to the opening where the farmers emptied their milk churns, she heard Helena laughing. Her father was laughing as well. A strange laugh, not like when he listened to *Take the Floor* on the wireless. She stopped. Something naughty was going on.

'No, Jesus, Matt, ah no. Ah don't.' Helena's laughter was brimming with excitement, 'Ah Matt, ah Jesus, that's below the belt.' Then silence.

'Dinny will catch us,' she was now saying. Deirdre crept closer.

'He can't,' her father said. 'I sent him to the village. Don't I think of everything.'

'You bastard.' Silence again, and then another cry from Helena: 'O God.'

Her heart pounding, Deirdre peeped in and waited for her eyes to grow used to the dim light. In a corner, her father was pressed up against Helena. One arm was around her neck, the other buried in her frock. She was pushing him away but he grabbed her again.

Deirdre turned, and rested her forehead against the cool cement wall. For a moment she feared they would hear the thumping of her heart. Crows were making a racket in the trees around the parochial house. A shotgun blast went off. Panic seized her. She began to back away towards the road, as if she'd done something wrong, then she ran. One strap of her schoolbag slipped off her shoulder, but she kept running.

Despite the pain in her stomach, she went to school the following day, slouching about on her own in the playground at the 12 o'clock break, and then pretending to join the games when her mother and the other teachers were taking their after-lunch stroll.

'I had my way of coping – like all children,' she told O'Brien.

'A sudden end to your childhood.'

'It's not something I like talking about. In any case, I never saw any of this as important – that is, until recently.'

After that incident, she had begun to make links: Mam and Dad in separate beds. One morning during the summer holidays from Oak Hill, she lay counting the tongue-and-groove ceiling laths of her bedroom to banish from her head the sound of her parents' shouting. 'I didn't go near her,' he was saying.

'Why did she pack her bags then? Why did she tell me she wouldn't stay another night in the house?'

'I don't know, Frances.'

'It was the same with Eileen. I'm telling you now, if another maid complains I'm going to Father Griffin.'

Rocking back and forth, Deirdre squatted one night at the turn of the stairs, while down below in the kitchen her mother and father dug up every injury from the past. Owen came and sat beside her. 'Dee Dee, Mam and Dad won't separate like Mr and Mrs Morgan,' he reassured her. 'The Morgans are Protestants from England. Catholics can't separate.'

During her final-year retreat at Oak Hill, she listened closely to the devil-at-dances priest when he gave the talk on vocations. 'Young ladies,' he intoned in the half-light of a September evening, 'this world is only a passing fancy. Dedicate your beautiful lives to Our Lord and Saviour. Become a bride of Christ. For that, you will enjoy the protection of the sinless Virgin Mary and receive life everlasting when you die.' After Benediction, she prayed before the stained-glass window to Saint Francis that if God helped Dad to stop going after other women, she would enter the noviciate.

She felt great. Free. Like being in the state of grace after a good Confession. This is the way to live, she thought, the way that pleases God most – as the priest said. Safe from shouting and lying, and praying in the dark at the turn of the stairs. As Head Girl that year, she shared a room with two prefects, and while the other two were saving up for Ricky Nelson records, she was reading Butler's *Lives of the Saints*. St Marie Goretti, who defended her virginity till death, became her favourite.

O'Brien suggested they go for a cup of coffee in the Killiney Court Hotel.

'If I didn't have a deeper conviction than just that childish one, I'd have left long ago,' she said, when they were seated in the lounge.

'Perhaps.'

'What do you mean, "Perhaps"?'

'You would always be connected to him by virtue of the sacrifice. In fact, joined to him for life.'

When the waitress arrived, he ordered a double brandy and made to get something for her, but she raised her hand. 'Coffee will be fine.' She hated what she was hearing: his dogmatic tone; the way he looked at her. He was back lecturing first-years in the seminary.

'What are you saying?' she asked.

'To some extent you would always be in that privileged place on his shoulders on your way to the Munster Final. Every time you reviewed your vocation, Deirdre, during retreats or times of crisis – like now – he would be in the picture.' He was plunging in a sword. 'And then entering a convent meant that Dad would never have any opposition – except for Jesus.'

'That doesn't make sense.'

'Sense? I wonder at times about sense. Over the years, I've listened to a goodly number describe their vocation. I often think it has as much to do with attachment to a father or mother as with this mysterious call.'

'Like in my case.'

'More so with priests. Falling to pieces as soon as Mammy dies, or leaving the priesthood and getting married before the flowers have withered on her grave.' His own mother had spent the last five years of her life with him at the parochial house. 'Where are you going? What time will you be back?' she used to ask him. 'You're like a gramophone record,' he'd say in reply. 'Easy for you to laugh, but you know I worry about you. I can't sleep until I hear you come in.'

For a few days O'Brien's words left a bad taste in her mouth. Despite his honours and his theology, what was he now without his brandy glass? No wonder he had been passed over for a diocese. But as her brain cooled, she began to mull over what he had said. She took the maroon jewellery box from her wardrobe and laid the bracelet on her desk. The years dissolved. Sundays listening to Micheál O'Hehir, and the look of delight on Dad's face when O'Connell the islandman was leaping like a gazelle around Croke Park. And when they won, he waltzed with her around the kitchen to his own music:

> Oh the days of the Kerry dances,
> Oh the ring of the piper's tune.

O'Brien was right. There could never be anyone to match Dad.

Coming up to Lent, Hannah was busy posting her Assertiveness Course on the noticeboard and distributing flyers. Joan was the first to put her name down. She was elated at breakfast one morning, after the previous night's session. It was wonderful, she told Deirdre. *The Inner Child*. Fantastic. 'This is right into my barrow. I can't get enough of it.' Life was never better; she was now going for a massage once a week to a lovely young man on the Stillorgan Road.

'Will you go?' she asked Deirdre.

'For a massage?' Deirdre laughed.

'No. Hannah's course. She has a few more places left.'

'I'd like to, Joan, but I don't have the time.'

'You should, you know. It's great. There are so many wonderful things about ourselves that we discover. And Hannah is top-drawer.'

A few days later, she was in floods of tears when she knocked on Deirdre's door. Sister Emmanuel had refused her permission to take a year off and go to Spokane. 'We can't afford to be without another Precious Blood in the school,' the Sister had told her. 'We need a presence in Oak Hill.'

'I'd set my heart on it,' Joan said. 'Hannah tells me it's what I need right now.'

'Control yourself.' Deirdre looked across at Joan's rounded shoulders quivering as she cried into her handkerchief. They could have paid a substitute: another exercise in showing who was boss. A replica of what she'd seen many times.

Joan dried her eyes and affected a smile: 'God's will.'

Deirdre looked away.

'I've no choice but to accept,' said Joan.

'Have you not?'

Joan stopped crying and looked her straight in the eye. 'No, Deirdre. I need the convent. I'd never make it in the world.'

'Others have.'

'Not me. Convents are hiding places for social misfits like me. You might think I've learned nothing from all these visits to doctors and counsellors.' She was clear-headed now. 'When you're not wanted as a child, it's doubtful if any counsellor can make much headway. No one can put Humpty Dumpty together again.' She laughed at her own comparison. 'Not even all the king's men.' The smile died. 'My mother – may God forgive her – never let me forget that I was one too many. The last of the litter. I would never have thought of marriage. Becoming a nun made me special, but that too wears off.'

'The Old Girls? They're tougher than old boots,' was de Chantal's reply when Deirdre sounded her out on the biography.

'I wouldn't like to cause them upset, especially by including what's in those diaries. I know I should have thought of this before.'

'If you think they would keel over because of a book, think again. And anyway, so much for spirituality, if they can't accept what is human. For too long we've all been cleaning the outside of the cup.' But despite reassurances from de Chantal and Maeve, Deirdre returned to the National Library and read over her typescript before she set about pruning.

Walking up Clare Street one day, she noticed an ungainly figure rummaging through the second-hand books in front of Greene's. Even in a light blue dress and pink cardigan instead of the habit, Peggy's awkward gait and the old-fashioned way she clutched her handbag were tell-tale signs that stretched back to their Oak Hill days. Surprised by Deirdre, she blushed and, as always, kept closing her eyes while she spoke. 'Look,' she said, holding up a paperback. *The Dynamics of Love.* Do you remember when you'd have to wait your turn for weeks before it was available in Oak Hill? Now it's going for 30p.'

'If you're not in a rush,' Deirdre suggested, 'you might like to join me for lunch.' They had entered the same year and been through a regime of strict obedience and much self-denial. The convent rules had had the effect of bonding them together like members of a family who have survived the vagaries of parents yet, when they meet, rake over bittersweet memories.

Peggy had kept up contact with Joan, who had filled her in on the sale of the land, the reinterment and other bits of news. They talked about the biography and Ita's death as they made their way towards Grafton Street. 'She kept us going in the tough times. Do you remember the French beds she used to make in the noviciate?' Peggy fumbled in her handbag, and proffered coins wrapped in a five-pound note at the cash register in the carvery, but Deirdre wouldn't hear of it.

They took their trays to a table and settled down to a salad, small talk and, eventually, Rita. 'She hasn't changed,' Peggy said. She laughed and closed her eyes. 'I was on sabbatical for a year, so in October of that year I had to sign the dispensation or return.' The smile died. 'It was like the death of someone belonging to me, you know what I mean?'

Deirdre nodded.

'I was slow about signing, but Rita says: "Come on now, Peggy, you've made your decision." I cried all the way back to Artane on the bus. "Did your Mammy die or somethin', love?" a woman beside me asked.'

She had a job supervising a community project – cleaning up a graveyard out near Malahide. 'It's the best I can get, Deirdre. No one wants you at my age, and I haven't the energy to go back into a classroom.' She had a nice little flat and was near the church and the library. Readjusting the bridge of her glasses, she rummaged again in her bag and drew out a dog-eared envelope. 'Here,' she said. 'I wrote to Rita for help.'

Deirdre read the reply:

Dear Peggy,

Thank you for your letter seeking financial assistance from the congregation. I am delighted to know that you are engaged in community development and that you are remaining loyal to the Gospel message. It must please you so much to be living near a church. The Lord always takes care of us, his special ones.

I have made representation on your behalf to the Superior General and she has reminded me of how generous the Precious Blood congregation has been towards you since you left us.

When you left us you received £4,000 and a further gratuity. Although in justice we were not required to do so, we furnished your flat in Artane with a TV, a bed, blankets and linen, kitchen furniture and two fireside chairs.

In conscience, Peggy, I feel we have fulfilled our duties towards you.

Kind regards in JC,
Sister Rita.

She took back the letter. 'And to think of the way I always tried to please them. Driving Sisters here and there after school, over to Galway or down to Belgrave at weekends, and then typing up stupid position papers and reports of meetings until all hours.' She put Deirdre in mind of the morning she had slumped at her prie-dieu, and a nun behind her had panicked: 'Oh sweet Jesus.' Her cry had woken the sleepy chapel. 'Sister Fides is dead.'

'Will you be able to manage?'

She brightened. 'I have a chance of getting a job as a secretary in the new comprehensive school they're building. Between ourselves,' her voice became hushed, 'I don't like this project thing. The boys are very rough, and their language is so coarse.' But she was over the worst of it now, she said – the fear of living on her own, meeting electricity and telephone bills. And then the shouts out in the street when the pubs closed.

'But I've made nice friends at the bridge club in Raheny. And I have coffee with Josephine every Saturday morning in the Kylemore. I met her one day at the bookstall in the Pro-Cathedral. She was like myself, except that she had left only two days before and was looking for a good B&B. We stayed together in a bedsit off the North Circular Road, but decided to look for our own place after a few weeks. We are all very set in our ways, Deirdre, especially after being in the convent for so long.'

'We are.'

Peggy had to catch a bus for Artane, but the two women said they would keep in contact.

Back in the National Library, Deirdre found herself reading the same sentence over and over again. Peggy's pathetic attempts at meeting someone took over: dancing in the Regency and the guard who took her up to the Phoenix Park and took out a packet of 'those dirty things, Deirdre.' On the sly, he had begun to lower the back of her seat, until she screamed. He dropped her at the nearest bus stop.

Deirdre gathered up her notes and switched off the green desk lamp. When she returned to Oak Hill, an envelope containing a draft of a mission statement for the millennium was waiting for her on the hall table. Clipped to the sheet was a note: 'Cast your eye over this and tell me what you think. We'll catch up later. Rita.'

She scanned the mission statement:

To create a caring and just environment where the unique qualities of every individual Sister is respected.

To nurture a spirit of mutual concern for present members and those who have elected to live the secular life.

To constantly renew our commitment to the outcasts of society in the spirit of our founder, Catherine Browne.

She stopped reading and threw the document in her bag. In her room, she glanced over the draft again, tore it in shreds and pitched it into the wastepaper basket.

O'Brien's experience with college theses was helpful when she was editing the biography. But his growing cynicism saddened her. When they had finished working, she had to endure bouts of intellectual pride or general discontent: one day it was the conservative Pope, another day it was young priests. 'Look,' he said, taking a letter of freedom from the bunch of marriage papers on his desk, 'a chap who is an expert at the computer, and he doesn't know the difference between *aliquo similiter libero* and *aliqua similiter libera*. Then there's another fellow, ordained five or six years, and he has a row of dolls and Snoopy toys on his mantelpiece. And he's in charge of the marriage-advisory council down here. I called to his house one evening; he was watching *Blue Peter*.'

He was in a bad mood that day; another one of the clique had been made auxiliary bishop. 'He has worn paths to Rome for the past twelve months since the vacancy occurred. No wonder there's so much talk about low morale in the clergy. The best have left, Deirdre. And the rest are only hanging on by their fingertips. Would you believe, one of my ordination year buys a fistful of

Lotto tickets every week? He'll be off if his numbers come up '

She had grown used to it; indeed, she was beginning to see that his fits of pique were justified.

And the more he drank, the more he retreated to an unfinished war with his parents. 'Every one of us had to do well.' As soon as they had eaten, his father, the Master, conducted classes, supervised their homework and surveyed the lessons for the following day, so that they would be ahead of the rest; then the Rosary and bed. One became a judge; two, nuns, one of whom crashed the convent car after drinking a bottle of wine. She left a month later for Chicago, where she had many strings to her bow.

'Each of us, of course, came out first in the exams. The *Sligo Champion* printed the results and the Master took the paper to Bundoran to be one up on the others. A lot of teachers went on their holidays to Donegal in those days. Another bite at the cherry through their children's success.' He chuckled and sipped his drink. 'Larkin was right about parents, Deirdre:

They fill you with the faults they had
And add some extra, just for you.'

They were delighted when he entered the seminary laden with every prize offered that year for the Leaving Certificate. 'It continued while I was in Maynooth – teachers' conferences – wherever. All they needed was a rosette and a parade ring.'

On Good Friday night, she decided to go to the Pro-Cathedral. A few of them had gone the year before, and were glowing afterwards. 'As good as being at Taize,' one of them had said. This year she would go alone. She was slipping away from the fold, but she wanted to make one last effort before a final decision. Two of the cars had been booked, and Bríd had assumed ownership of the Starlet. So from the top of the Enniskerry bus, she watched the world slip by. The red-brick houses of Merrion Road were at their best in the slanting sun, and the trees were sprouting after the summer weather of the previous few days. While the bus was stopped outside the RDS, a gust of wind threw into confusion a drift of cherry blossoms on the footpath and a swirl of pink snow floated up into the air.

In the candlelit cathedral, she took a leaflet from the table near the door and slipped into one of the seats at the back. Spotlights drew attention to the white marble altar. With a conductor's flowing movement of her hand, the chanter was encouraging the congregation to join in the singing; from overhead came the heavy tones of the organ in the lead-in:

> *Jesus, remember me when you come into your kingdom.*
> *Jesus, remember me when you come into your kingdom.*

Clerical students in soutane and surplice were lifting a black cross into position in the sanctuary. One of them pranced around whispering and directing with stylised gestures until the base of the enormous cross had settled in its stand; then, with a flourish, he draped the cross-beam with a white cloth. The sanctuary was cold and bare and lonely. Christ was dead on this night. A woman in the seat ahead was squinting at the hymn-sheet. Deirdre glanced at her face, and at the lines of stress and the furrows of disappointment at each side of her mouth. Yet she envied her involvement. After a while the candles began to blur and a strange feeling stole up on her, accompanied by the discomforting rise of heat to her neck and then her face. Misty images of other Good Fridays took shape: dark brown Stations of the Cross at Clogher

Church, her mother with a black-covered prayer book; the chapel at Oak Hill. All now seemed to be dissolving in a swirl like water down a plughole.

When the tears began to flow, she placed her elbows on the armrest and shaded her face with her hands. She cried right through the ceremony, until a woman beside her whispered: 'Excuse me.' They were going up to kiss the feet of the crucified Jesus. Deirdre let the woman go by, but didn't join the procession.

A few of the nuns were still in the chapel when she returned to Oak Hill. Now calm, she revisited her upset. She could no longer regard the struggles of the previous months as dry prayer – as one of those valleys that God is supposed to send to test perseverance. Good Friday was a prophet's battle against the forces of evil – a battle that would result in victory two days later. And she was the recipient of a myth that had provided a solid frame for millions against the dread of sickness and loss and death; and against life's conundrums. It bespoke the hopes and aspirations of all who crave for justice and who want good to triumph. Easter Sunday is the supreme happy ending. Jesus promises light at the end of the tunnel. One sultry May morning, she, a child of seven, had received the whole mystery on her tongue. Now the mystery had become a thin disc of unleavened bread. Maybe the Jesus story would charm her back again one day. But not now.

Still she searched through the spiritual books that had never failed her in the past: the collected works of John of the Cross and the writings of Julian of Norwich. Scanning through *The Cloud of Unknowing* she came across a note inserted by herself; it was a quotation from Jung, dated July 1983, during her thirty days' retreat at Manresa:

> But we cannot live the afternoon of life according
> to life's morning: for what in the morning was true
> will in the evening have become a lie.

The steering committee, headed by Rita, called together the congregation for a Saturday seminar on the mission statement. Again the retired nuns in the country availed of their free-transport allowance to spend a weekend in Dublin, and renew their attachment to Oak Hill.

Hannah had the overhead projector in place; for each article of the mission statement, she had produced an acetate sheet. One Sister was glad to invest energy in this person-centred statement. 'We are now being really proactive,' she announced. 'We need Process.'

'Sisters,' said Hannah, 'we in the steering committee welcome feedback, so it's now open to the house.' Light from the projector exaggerated her bulk and cast a monstrous shadow on the wall. 'Well, I think,' said a nun whose earrings dangled when she spoke, 'it gives us an opportunity to use our feminine qualities to minister to each other and journey together.' Hannah nodded while the woman spoke. 'And also a way of being Church,' the woman continued. They broke into clusters and appointed a secretary to report to the plenary session. The Angelus bell rang out in a nearby church; some of the old nuns blessed themselves, but most were lost in the Process.

During the final session, Joan stood up, despite Rita's attempts to silence her. 'We don't have any more time, Joan – some of the Sisters have to catch a train. We'll take your points and deal with them at the steering committee.'

'No, you won't,' Joan said, and referred to one of the handouts. '"A just environment which respects the unique qualities of every

Sister."' She laughed – a mocking cackle that set everyone on edge. 'Who are we fooling?' Gaining confidence now, she looked around the room. 'How many have ever felt unique? How many have ever felt their qualities were respected? Well, not me, for one.'

'Joan,' Rita appealed, 'we haven't much time. We want to wrap it up.'

'Not much time,' she chortled. 'There's never any time. No one has time any more. So whatever happened to all the "quality time" we're supposed to be sharing, then?' She returned to the handout: 'Listen to this. This is rich: "To nurture a spirit of mutual concern for present members and those who have elected to live the secular life".' Rita had turned away and was biting the inside of her lip.

'Eleven were professed with me.' Joan now became aware of the startling effect her outburst was having; her voice trembled, yet she continued. 'How many times have any of these been invited back? Has anyone written to find out if they are dead or alive?' She began to weep.

'Yes,' said Rita, standing up, 'Joan has brought to our notice some salutary reminders. Thanks for sharing, Joan. And now we'll have to wrap it up.'

'She's high again this weather,' Deirdre remarked to de Chantal while they strolled around the cloister. The nuns from the country were getting taxis to take them to the train station.

'Joan isn't as loopy as they would like to think.'

'Did you notice the numbers were down again?' Deirdre asked.

'We've heard it all before.' But de Chantal was more interested in the biography. 'What's the state of play?'

'I'm deleting the controversial parts.'

'Why?'

'Cowardice, perhaps. Rita has a point: Catherine has been

through enough, without her memory being plastered all over the newspapers. Guilt, too.' Some weeks before, she had been watching an old black-and-white film made in Elphin by an American film company. 'Someone from the crew of the *Quiet Man,* I believe. It must have been done back in the fifties. You know – the full habit.' She had listened to the Old Girls talking about the nuns who had appeared in the film. The work they did – teaching, nursing and, when their day's labour was done, cleaning the classroom and the convent. Training choirs for the Feis Cheoil. Camera-shy locals with gap-toothed smiles gave glowing testimonies to the Precious Blood Congregation. The town, they said, had been decimated by emigration, but no one was turned away from the convent door. They got anything from blankets to chickens to a few potatoes from the garden.

'It's easy to rejig things and delete whatever might seem to give a poor likeness,' Deirdre commented. 'It was never going to sell more than five hundred copies, so it won't be a great loss to historical research.'

'A pity,' said de Chantal.

Deirdre had more on her mind than the biography the next time she met O'Brien. 'Did you ever find yourself without a compass?' she asked him.

'Welcome to the human race.'

'But it's as if I've to rethink the whole thing out from the beginning. I've nothing except my health and my training as a teacher. I can't pray. But what's even more unsettling is that I don't *want* to pray.'

She related the events of the night in the Pro-Cathedral. 'The liturgy of Holy Week used to mean so much. But that night and ever since . . . ' She shook her head. 'I can't remain in this position for the rest of my life, so after this launch I'm going to apply for a sabbatical.'

'For how long?'

'A year, two years. Maybe I'll sign the dispensation form long before then.'

The launch of her book was held one Sunday in Browne Hall, where Deirdre, as Head Girl, had once read the Proclamation for de Valera. Again, overnighters from the country and from other convents in Dublin swelled their ranks. After lunch, they strolled around the grounds while they waited for the guests to arrive, and when the first raindrops fell they hurried for shelter beneath the ambulatory, where they discussed summer holidays and the appointment of lay principals to their schools. One nun, who had put many an inspector in his place, had a plan for ensuring they got the right candidate. She told her captive audience: 'In an interview board of five, always have three on your side. Otherwise you'd end up with a crackpot.' They nodded. She had a reputation for running the best school north of the Liffey. Each morning she had stood at the school gate checking her watch as the teachers hurried by.

Belgrave was also a topic of conversation. Very soon it would appear in the *Irish Times* Property Section, Rita told another group. She was glad to say that an American software company was still interested. She put a finger to her lips. 'We have to be careful about this one. There's need for another access road, which means knocking a few old trees. We'll have to move fast, or those loony eco-warriors will be on top of us.' The house was a listed building, and the land had been rezoned for development. 'A few thousand or so to Concern, and then we'll sell by public tender, so no one will know what we get. But first we have to make sure we publicise the donation.'

At the centre of the hall, on the polished floorboards, stood a lectern and a microphone. Nearby on a table were stacks of *Catherine Browne: A Seeker for Justice*. The cover showed a cameo of the founder, connected by rays to pictures of convents and hospitals in different parts of the world.

The associates of Precious Blood who attended funerals sat around with glasses of wine and cocktail snacks. Priests from Dundrum and Churchtown, as well as those who had friends among the community, turned up as well. Again, the Old Girls reminded Aidan Doyle how he had been their best chaplain. Millar steered one of the younger nuns to a corner. Owen and Julia and some of the family had travelled from Kerry.

After Richard O'Brien's opening address, Sister Emmanuel spoke about Catherine's courage, and how she had stood up to political systems. Her integrity, the Sister said, was an inspiration for all women, especially those who had chosen to follow her. 'She was a feminist in the best sense of the word.' Her speech was well prepared, like an essay that might please her teacher, but it was a standard eulogy, laced with hackneyed commendations. From her script, she read: 'Catherine was a woman who combined a love for the poor with a recognition that young Catholic women of the last century would receive a good education in their own country.

'Deirdre,' she said, 'has demonstrated, not for the first time, her exceptional writing skill and, in a short length of time, has produced a work that will be a valuable sourcebook for students of history.' Even after a determined effort, she losing her audience. The tell-tale signs of boredom appeared: someone stifled a yawn and brushed her hand along her hair; another let her gaze wander off into the swaying trees outside the window. Proud of the new shoes she had bought the day before in Cripps's sale, a nun began to curve and arch her foot, admiring her purchase. But they all applauded vigorously when the speech had ended.

'Congratulations,' said de Chantal, when they found a quiet moment after the rest had gone. 'It's just as well. Let sleeping dogs lie. How you succeeded in making it interesting after that editing, I'll never fathom.'

'Thanks, de Chantal,' Deirdre said.

They walked around by the lake, where the chestnuts and oaks were heavy with fresh leaves.

'You remember when you told me about the diaries?' Deirdre looked at her old teacher. 'And you thought we had moved on and were ready to accept what was censured in the past.'

'Yes, I know.'

'I've been doing some rethinking. Not just this sort of tunnel vision – other things. I'll tell you about it another time.'

They fell into an awkward silence. 'Before the news gets out, de Chantal, I want you to know I've applied for a year's sabbatical.'

'This is what I dreaded. Why are you going?'

'Different reasons. Discovering what brought me here in the first place. The reaction to the book. But I know I could weather these.' They stopped walking and Deirdre faced de Chantal. 'Whatever it is I'm looking for, I can't find here.'

'If that's what God wants.' De Chantal touched her arm. 'In a way it's funny. You're being tipped to succeed Emmanuel at the next Chapter.'

'There mightn't be any election. She has let it be known that she has changed her mind about stepping down – so Rita told someone.'

'Didn't take her long to forget her beloved Nigeria. Shows what power does.' But de Chantal was only interested in Deirdre's decision. 'It's a big step. Are you sure?'

'No. But I have to know, one way or the other. To be truthful, I'm scared. Except for the few years in America and my sojourn in Mespil Road, Oak Hill has been my life since I was thirteen. And to face the music at this stage in my life . . . '

'I'll miss you.' The heavy silence was broken only by the sound of their footsteps in the deserted cloister. De Chantal's brave effort to be strong failed. After a while she removed her glasses and dried her eyes. Deirdre too took some time to compose herself. 'By the way – I couldn't tell you this before – it's largely because of my decision to leave that I caved in on the book.'

'I don't follow.'

'If I were staying, I'd put up a fight. But they can have it, if that's their notion of truth, or courage, or whatever goes for spirituality. I'm surprised at Emmanuel. I thought there was more to her. She's probably as big a control freak as the rest of them.'

'May God direct you.' De Chantal's voice trailed off as Bríd drove up in the Starlet; she lowered the window. 'I'm off to see *Dancing at Lughnasa.*, she said, grinning as she eased the car into gear. Don't wait up for me.'

Waiting in line with other flat-hunters in Leeson Park one evening, she overheard a conversation between three young women. In a good-humoured way, they were complaining about a ward sister.

'A blue-arsed fly every Monday because of all the operations,' said one.

Her copper-haired friend diagnosed the problem. 'A shag, that's what she needs.'

'Do her all the good in the world.'

They flitted over other interests: a nursing colleague was getting married, three others were going to Australia for a year, and the new intern in St Lawrence's Ward was a hunk. They became skittish and spoke above a whisper: fragments like 'blow job' and 'with handcuffs' reached her. Later on they were headed for Temple Bar.

Many of the flats were grotty: stains on the mattresses, the inside showing through tears in the material. In other places, the smell of cigarette smoke and beer or a stench from the bathroom lingered in the air. In some, water dripped from the taps. She eventually found a second-floor apartment in Elgin Road.

She met Rita in the corridor one day when she was removing clothes and other pieces in Hannah's Nissan. 'You could knock me over with a feather, Deirdre, when I heard the news.' She was close to tears. 'I thought you would be the last person. Had it anything to do with the book? I mean, I was only saying what I thought.'

'Nothing, Rita. Nothing to do with that.'

'What will you do? God love you.'

Deirdre told her about the vacancy in Mespil Road and how Sister Emmanuel had offered her Oak Hill.

'Oh.' Rita reddened.

'I'll probably take Mespil Road.'

'Good choice. I always say it's best when we leave to go somewhere else. Turn over a new leaf. If there's anything I can do – removing boxes, anything – just let me know. I have to dash. We'll meet up before you go.' She was already backing away.

During the transition, Deirdre's radio sounded hollow in the bare room: fresh patches on the wall showed where her pictures had hung. Clothes hangers dangled when she opened the press. She stayed out of the convent as much as possible and had lunch on a couple of occasions with Maeve; afterwards the two of them strolled through St Stephen's Green or did a walkabout in Trinity College. She had much to tell Maeve about her meeting with the Superior General and her interview for the vacant post at Mespil Road. 'The following day I had a phone call from the principal saying I'd got it,' Deirdre said.

The day she visited O'Brien, he was on his knees putting down lobelia and marigolds at the front of the house. Locking her car near a wicket gate, she caught the sound of a tractor engine. Downhill, a green harvester was showering silage into a trailer; crows were swooping and searching the shorn field for gleanings. The glorious smell of cut grass carried in the breeze.

'You'll be able to read Plato while you get a suntan,' she said to him, indicating his new conservatory. Her survey took in the high rise of his three-storey house.

'It used to be a land agent's house. We took over from the Raj, Deirdre.' He followed her gaze. 'After Catholic emancipation, the natives wanted their priest to match the landlord. I found a notebook from around 1860 showing the hard-earned few shillings that went to buy this mausoleum. Around the time bishops were trying to tame Catherine Browne.'

Before she went shopping to Rathdrum, his housekeeper had left out two salads covered in cling film on the kitchen table.

'Did they look after you all right?' he asked, while opening a bottle of wine.

'Better than I expected. To be fair, things have changed since Peggy's day. I could have bought a car, but I decided to put the extra into the flat. I'll have my salary in September, so I'll manage until then.'

'I admire your courage, although if I had predicted who would part company with the Precious Blood Sisters, you wouldn't have been at the top of the list.'

'At times I feel as if a burden has been lifted – you know, that I'm free. Then again, I'm not sure. Am I just menopausal? Or is it the panic of the closing door?' She gave a nervous laugh. 'At times, it's like a dream I can't wake from.'

'Was it Ita's death?' he asked, when they were seated at the table.

'Ita's death, visiting the hospital, seeing all that sickness. Then others bailing out. One of my group told me she didn't want to spend the few precious years God had given her in a sinking ship.' She explained that what discouraged her more than anything was the way they closed ranks; even the Superior General. 'I had hopes when she was elected, after her work in Africa. One thing's for sure, she's grown to like her bit of power.' Putting the jigsaw together gave her a different perspective also, she said. 'I often hear them saying: "I'm not staying for the reasons I entered." The irony of my situation is that I'm leaving because of the reasons I entered.'

'Still, those that discover their hidden motives don't always have the courage of their convictions.' He leaned back and cast a defeated look among the headstones. 'I should have gone years ago. A hostage to fortune. Seminary professor at thirty-four, and greater things to come if I played the game. If you'll pardon the expression, it was a turn-on – like sex. Then one day you begin to ask, what's it all for? No one there by your side, no children to watch as they grow, open their minds to books.' But he stopped himself. 'The ramblings of an old man, Deirdre.'

The red wine swirled when he refilled their glasses. He brightened. 'You know best what to do with your life. And you're not too late to meet someone.'

'Hold on, now. Give me time to catch my breath,' she laughed. 'One thing's for sure, I'll not be going to the singles dancing in the Regency like poor Peggy.' She didn't think her life would change that much. 'In some ways it will be more isolated: in Oak Hill there was always company. But at least I won't be a taxi driver when I'm finished my day's work.'

'You're joking.' Aidan Doyle studied her with boyish amazement when she told him she was leaving.

'I'm taking a year's sabbatical.' She explained what had led up to her decision.

He collected himself, and then set about trying to dissuade her with his version of sound thinking. 'Could you not do like, well, others. Nowadays, people like us can have both without any fuss. What's wrong with having the best of both worlds? Sure, we're harming no one.'

She looked at him for a moment: contempt gave way to pity. 'I'm not "others". And anyway, the sexual side is only a small part of it.'

She started again but he was on a different track. 'The way I see it, Deirdre, is this: we're human and we're only doing what's in our nature.'

'Well, regarding that. You knew all along I was unhappy with the way we were carrying on.'

'Yes, but for all your high morals, you didn't object too much at the beginning.'

'True.'

'Sorry, I didn't mean that.'

'We have a different way of looking at things, Aidan.'

The wounded look on her face caused him to regret his outburst. His tone softened. 'I find it hard to see how the odd lapse is that bad. I mean, we'll be long enough dead, God knows.'

'And that's more or less why I'm going. That and other reasons.'

'What?'

'We'll be long enough dead.'

Her bolt from the blue caused him to become confessional in a maudlin way. For the first ten or twelve years of his priesthood, he had kept the rule. During that time as an emigrant chaplain in London, he had fallen in love with a nurse from the Royal Brampton Hospital, and when he wouldn't go back on his ordination promises, she broke it off with him.

'I didn't blame her,' he explained. 'She was full of life. I did her wedding in Thurles, and then took to the bed for a week.' And while he tossed and turned, he decided he had done enough self-denial for the rest of his life. 'Even though I don't keep the rules, I'd be a fish out of water without the church. Millar is the same. First Communion day. The bishop coming for Confirmations. Holy Week. It's ingrained in us by now, Deirdre. Meeting the lads for golf and the craic on a Thursday. And I don't have any problems about faith, thank God.' He hesitated. 'Blokes I've known since the seminary days know now that celibacy won't change in our lifetime. So if we want to stay in, we've little option.' He stopped and looked at her. 'Will this change things between us, then?'

'I need time, Aidan.'

'Am I barred from Elgin Road?'

'I think you will respect my wish. I need time.'

The boyish look reappeared. 'Sure, maybe we'll run into each other, anyhow.'

'I'm sure we will.'

The holiday season was a godsend when she was leaving Oak Hill. Many of the retired Sisters who had Motherd the working nuns, keeping their dinners warm when they returned from school, were gone to other convents, or to houses by the sea. Before they left, they cried, embraced and made many promises of frequent meetings and prayers. 'And with God's help, Deirdre will be back again.'

Before going off with Chris for a weekend in Wales, Bríd dropped in with a kettle and a tin of Earl Grey. 'Only out of self interest,' she joked. 'I intend to be a frequent visitor on my way into town, so be warned.'

Hannah was busy with Zoe, preparing workshops on self-assertiveness for the autumn. She did, however, go with Deirdre to Elgin Road a couple of evenings and helped her with dusting, and moving armchairs and other pieces into place. Going in the car, she told her how she would have to put back her holidays until late August: 'Zoe and myself will manage a few days then.' They had a cup of tea afterwards in a Baggot Street café, where she assured Deirdre that the Nissan was hers while she was moving out.

A couple of evenings before she left, Deirdre sat with de Chantal in the community room. The holidaymakers had gone off to dream about Kilmainham Jail and Trinity College and all the places they had visited that day in the sightseeing bus. In so far as they could, they both took shelter from the harsh reality of parting by keeping to small talk such as the July Assembly to fill the doleful gaps. The Chapter would elect a new Superior General. 'Since you're not in the running, Rita has it all to herself now. God help us, we'll be lucky if she doesn't put us on the market. Luckily for most of us, we have exhausted our shelf-life. With God's help, Deirdre, you'll be back with us again.' De Chantal took their glasses to a side table, where a bottle of gin stood beside mineral water and soft drinks. 'One for the road,' she announced.

The old nuns had lit a fire with briquettes against the chill of a summer's evening; now the flames had eaten through the compressed layers, and from time to time the towers caved in. Red-hot coals glowed for a while and then turned to ashes. The room grew dim.

When the second drink began to take effect, de Chantal lost her grip. 'I know I shouldn't make it hard for you.' She removed her glasses and dried her eyes, and began to dust down old memories: anecdotes from the time when she had been in charge of the dormitories. A mother's fond memories of baby talk. One of the boarders' favourite pranks when they were wound up – such as before the holidays – was to close a girl into a trunk; then they spun her around the dormitory and she had to guess where she was. On one occasion Deirdre was the victim. After coming to rest, she waited in the darkness for the next move, but the dormitory had grown silent, apart from whispers and the scurrying of feet. Afraid they would leave her locked in, she called out, but got no reply; then she heard the testy voice of Mother Superior in the corridor: 'What's going on in there?'

'I'll look after that now, Mother,' de Chantal reassured her.

An insomniac, Mother Superior haunted the corridors at all hours. She now appeared in the dormitory and made straight for the source of the commotion. 'Who is causing the disturbance, Sister de Chantal?' she asked.

'Just a couple of girls who needed a drink of water, Mother, and they got nervous in the dark. Everything is under control now.'

'All right, Sister.' Turning, she noticed that the young nun was standing in front of a trunk.

'What is that doing there, Sister?'

'Oh, that, Mother. I'll take care of that now.'

'Goodnight then, Sister. *Benedicamus Domino*.'

'Amen. *Deo Gratias*, Mother.'

On her last morning, Deirdre is awake long before the alarm clock goes off. Joan clearing her throat in the next room breaks the early-morning silence: she is halfway through another Catherine Cookson.

So as not to wake the holidaymakers, Deirdre picks her steps along the corridor, avoiding the creaky spot near one of the connecting doors. Making her way down the wide staircase, she pauses to store away images of the rococo work on the walls and ceiling. 'Among the finest examples in the British Isles,' a curator had once told Mother Superior. Nuns showing around their guests had proudly quoted his words. Students of architecture, with notebooks and cameras, visited from time to time also. Along the ground corridor, she continues past the old prints framed in black: *Jesus at the Garden of Gethsemane* and *Jesus Meets the Women of Jerusalem*. In the chapel, she kneels at the back, beside the organ. She had resolved to avoid any mawkish sentiment on this morning, yet random scenes break to the surface: the heavy swell of the organ and the scent of Benediction, and a full chapel singing with one voice:

> *Salve Regina, Mater misericordiae;*
> *vita, dulcedo, et spes nostra, salve.*
> *Ad te clamamus*

But she pulls down the shutters, and takes a last look around before making her way to the front door, where she stands for a moment on the top step. Out beyond the Pigeon House, a thousand sequins dance on Dublin Bay. Already the traffic is getting steamed up on the Dundrum Road; a bus growls as it changes gear while passing the main gate. In the nunnery, a car alarm screams. She is now about to join this troubled stream: those who fret about bills and mortgages in the gridlock, balding husbands who steal glances at girls in their school uniforms, wives who collect stamps for the free tablemats in the local supermarket. Each Saturday she will dust and hoover, and on a Sunday, take the canal path to Haddington Road Church while nurses sleep off the effects of nights in Temple Bar with hunks from St Lawrence's Ward.

For a moment, the claw of doubt grips her heart. Maybe this is all a big mistake. Something to do with the change of life. Couldn't she do as Aidan Doyle had suggested – play the game like Bríd and others, who meet their friends at the weekend and go through the motions at assemblies and discerning exercises. And sing the praises of Process and the Enneagram.

But the cloud passes over; her decision is the right one. The tell-tale signs are enough to convince her of that. Despite tears and farewell hugs, she has come to know something like a breakthrough, as if for the first time she has taken some control of her life. The buried-alive dreams and the attacks of psoriasis have disappeared as well.

She goes down the steps mottled with lichen, and walks along by the row of lawn blocks. The fragrance of high summer rises from the cut grass. Yesterday a young man with ear mufflers and a red football shirt emblazoned with the word 'SHARP' had been speeding around on a tractor. He replaced Eddie, who after fifty-one years had been given his walking papers and a clock. She gazes at the columns that flank the front door, and a well-lit stage fills her head with something like scenes from a play. Going home for the long holidays. *Go Ye Afar* and the *Veni Creator* and Foley's funeral car – keepsakes now. Like the photos in the Long Parlour: sunny smiles and cream habits surrounded by high school kids in a tropical playground.

She follows the outer boundary of the walled garden and then along the laurel path. The cemetery has been trimmed; here and there lies a bunch of flowers near a black iron cross. The spare details in white paint show a Sister's name and the day she died. Drops of moisture cling to the cellophane around the chrysanthemums she had put on Ita's grave for her birthday. She blesses herself and walks on, pausing before the memorial to Sister Cecily and all missionaries who are buried in foreign soil. She casts her eye over the names of Catherine Browne and her reinterred companions on a clean stone.

To avoid drawn-out goodbyes and more tears, she had brought two bags and a briefcase down the back stairs and left them in one of the parlours while the holiday brigade were making an appearance in the corridors for Matins. The bulk of her belongings are now at Elgin Road. She still needs a few items: an ironing board, bookshelves, and a few odds and ends for the kitchen.

Two nuns from the Carrick-on-Shannon convent join her at a corner table for breakfast; de Chantal slides into the vacant place. At a nearby table an old nun is giving out about young people and how they drink to excess when they get their examination results. 'That's the Celtic Tiger for you. More money than sense,' she says. Deirdre braces herself for another wave of final good wishes and how she is the world's gain and the convent's loss, but the well-practised way of discretion comes into play. The merits of hot water first thing in the morning, the government minister who has a mistress and Clery's sale come to their rescue. Then, after eggshell hugs, they are gone and she is left with de Chantal.

'You're all set,' De Chantal says.

'Ready for the road.'

'Rita is taking you to your flat.'

'No. She had a phone call from the solicitor about Belgrave. Some problem about rezoning. She had to go off yesterday evening. But she was very apologetic and left me a cheque for two hundred pounds in an envelope. Maybe she's not the worst of them.'

Just before the taxi pulls up, Joan comes waddling down the corridor to join them at the front door. This isn't goodbye, they assure each other, and with God's help Deirdre will be back with them again when the year's sabbatical is up. But Joan breaks down. She will never forget Deirdre's kindness. 'What will I do now?' she sobs.

De Chantal puts an arm around her sloped shoulders. 'If it's God's will, Deirdre will be back with us again, Joan. There there, now.' She is back again in the dormitory calming the night fears and speaking in a soothing tone: 'We have to be strong, Joan. For all our sakes.'

Anxious to avoid another scene, Deirdre says: 'As soon as I get settled, we'll have a house-warming.' The driver glances at the three of them and closes down the car boot, and above the crackle of the taxi radio he tries to keep an ear to their conversation, but another call comes in.

The two nuns wave and the car disappears around the curve of the driveway.

'Great day, Missus,' says the driver. 'The forecast is promisin'.'

She eases back against the seat. 'That's good to hear, after the bad spell.'

'Yes.' He glances at her a second time in the mirror; he is anxious to talk. 'Things are pickin' up at last.' They wait at the convent gates to join the world.